SNOW

SNOW

Margaret Jones

Academy
Chicago
Publishers

Published in 1984 by
Academy Chicago, Publishers
425 N. Michigan Ave.
Chicago, IL 60611

Printed and bound in the USA

Library of Congress Cataloging in Publication Data

Jones, Margaret, fl. 1968–
    Snow.

    I. Title.
PR6060.O55S64   1984   823'.914   84-14600
ISBN 0-89733-115-X

C 3349

The boy said he had caught one on his hand. A snowflake. It settled on a roughened area of skin. 'Look,' he said, 'I've got one.'

'I've told you to come in and get your breakfast,' Della said. She was looking up at the sky. The boy looked up at the sky too and he closed his big hand.

Della said: 'You're to take those bales up to the barn, then cake the cows and feed the bull. And have you got the water yet?'

The boy felt at the moistness where the snowflake had melted in his palm. 'I've nearly got all the buckets filled,' he said, lying.

'*All* the buckets?'

He had been told to fill up every barrel, plastic bucket, jug and bowl he could lay hands on. He had been told that if the pipes froze up there would be no water and if there was no water, the animals would starve. Because he was lying, he made himself look straight into Della's face. 'I wouldn't let them cows and horses starve, Missus. If they starve, they'll die.' His hand chopped up and down in the cold air. 'I'll see to it that all them bowls and jugs are filled as well. You needn't worry, I'll do it for you.'

Della put out her own hand now, testing the thickness of the falling snow on her woollen glove. 'I don't care what the forecast says, this is here to stay. It's no good Mr Rixon trying to tell me it's just a snow flurry. He doesn't know what he's talking about.' She motioned to the boy: 'Come on, you'd better come inside and get your breakfast. You'll have to hurry up if you're going to get all that work done too. We'll be in Queer Street if the water freezes up.'

The boy thought of a picture he had seen on television. Ranchers rode doomed horses into Death Valley, into the sweltering California heat. The men lay down behind their

[5]

horses, trying to get some shade. There was no shade for the horses; they heaved and coughed, their whinnies weakened. The men's tongues were swollen and their skins blistered in the heat. The boy felt himself becoming frightened. He thought of the four hunters in the field, he thought how they were the only living things that Della valued, or so she said, and he thought how they might lie down and die because he had got no water for them. He wished that it were true that he had filled the buckets. He thought of the tongues of the old cows swelling like balloons and the name *Death Valley* rang in his head. He began to stammer: 'Missus, it won't be like that picture me and Hugh was watching, will it?' He coughed. 'You know, them horses' tongues all swollen up.'

But Della's mind was fixed on the falling snow. 'Daniel, why are you talking about television now?'

'Them horses' tongues in *Death Valley*. You know, you watched some of it with me and Hugh. Them horses and their tongues.'

But her whole attention was devoted to the falling snow. 'Sometimes I wish you'd hold your tongue.'

'Don't you remember? *Death Valley*? When they all burned up in the heat?'

'Heat?' Della said. 'Look, I honestly don't know what you're talking about.' She shook the snow from off her glove. 'Now, come inside and have your breakfast.'

'I'm not hungry,' the boy said, buying time so that he could make good his lie about the water.

'Of course you are. A boy of your age! You need your food, especially in this weather. Believe me, there'll be so much to do, it'll be a long time before we have time to eat again.'

'That's all I'm saying,' her husband told her son.

The boy leaned close to his dish of porridge; he had mixed treacle in it so that it had begun to turn bronze. It was not possible to see his face, he was so close to the mixture that his features were obscured.

[6]

'Daniel,' Della said. 'Will you please eat that porridge. You play about with your food as if you were a child. No one would suspect you were sixteen.'

He ate a spoonful of the mixture he had made. Della stood over him, but she was not really watching him, she was not even thinking about him. She was thinking: Why am I here with these strangers? My husband, my son, this boy? Why am I listening to this argument? Why don't I tell them that they must resolve it or bring it to an end? The words she was hearing she had heard in that kitchen again and again.

'And you two,' she said. 'I don't want to hear any more of this silly talk from either of you. You go out of your way to misunderstand each other—'

'Della,' Rixon said. 'This is a debate.'

'Debate?' The boy examined the word as if it were something entirely new to him. He reached with his spoon and dipped it once more into the treacle.

'Motion: Only my father's generation understands the meaning of the word "work",' Hugh said.

'Work.' The spoonful of treacle trickled into the porridge. 'Hugh says reading books is work.'

'If you don't hurry up, Daniel—'

'Counting pound notes is work too,' the boy said. 'Giving money to people in a bank.'

'And mowing down those gunmen,' Hugh said.

'Bank robbers, like that Sundance Kid. Did you see that picture, Hugh? Them two robbers, robbing all them banks?' The boy's knife became a gun, he shot at Rixon and then he shot at Hugh.

If only someone would, Della thought. If only someone would come along and shoot them down and set me free. Then she bit her lip to cancel out the thought. The boy trained the knife on Della, but at a look from her he lowered it.

'Them bank robbers, that Butch Cassidy. People like that, they don't care who they kill.'

If there had been no Rixon and no Hugh, things might have

[7]

been different, her whole life might have been different, she was thinking now. There would be no one to care for, no one to provide for, no one to worry her, no one to drain her resources away. She made herself smile at them all, she put two pieces of bacon on to a plate for the boy. There had only been six pieces to begin with, they had been cut by Rixon. Six for four people; what kind of logic was there there? She would have none herself, she would deny herself bacon in order to atone for her ungenerous thoughts. 'You men, you're always so aggressive, it's part of the way you're made.' She still smiled, watching them, watching their three pairs of male jaws moving. Outside the snow was coming down faster: faster and thicker against the window pane. Perhaps the snow would fall so thickly that it would not be possible for Hugh to leave. Perhaps he would have no choice but to stay for a day or two longer. A minute or two ago she had almost wanted to see him mown down, but now she found herself mouthing a silent prayer: Don't let him go. At the same time she wondered what ties of blood made her want him to stay. Why did human mothers want to hang on to their young? Why not kick them out and let them fend for themselves like birds did? Would a mother robin keep her son in clothes, food, drinks, petrol for his car, books, money to spend on girls? She sighed and then she tried to turn the sigh into a cough in case they heard it. Because of the hot steam from the stove and because of the bitter air outside, the window had become misted. She leaned forward and she wrote in the mist half of the name 'Eugene', then hastily, so that no one could read it, she scrubbed it out.

'I bet I *could* rob your old bank,' the boy was warning Rixon. 'It'd be dead easy. I could rob it, if I had a stocking and a gun.'

'Daniel, I shan't tell you again,' Della said. But her words were automatic, they were said without volition, spoken with no intent.

'Tell you what. I could borrow your old twelve bore. I could saw it down. Then I could put the stocking on my head.' He mopped up his egg yolk with a piece of bread; his two pieces of bacon remained untouched.

[8]

Wasted! she thought.

If Eugene had lived, there would have been no Rixon and no Hugh and there would have been no boy. If Eugene had lived she would not have had to listen to the arguments between her husband and her son, she would never have felt lonely and deserted as she did now. If Eugene had lived, there would have been no need to tolerate this intolerable boy. She half closed her eyes, visualizing their three places, empty of them.

'I could shoot all of you: pow, pow, pow, pow!' the boy said.

'What complete and utter nonsense,' she heard her own voice say.

Rixon threaded a brown lace into his black shoe.

'Brown laces, black shoes,' he said. 'Well, at least the contrast makes it easy on the failing eyes.'

He laid the shoe next to the other one on the mat at the side of their bed.

'Poor Tom,' Della said.

'Why "poor"? Why did you say "poor"?'

'I don't know.' *Poor* because he had to go and earn his living at the bank when he would rather stay here at the farm and play at being a farmer. *Poor* because he had a wife who did not remember to buy black laces for his black shoes. 'I don't know why I said it. Anyway, come on, let's go. You've still got to feed that bull before you put your shoes on. That's one chore I'm not taking on.' Following him down the narrow, twisting stairs, she leaned forward and rested a hand upon his shoulder gently, spacing the distance between them in the poor light. She could hear the boy's voice outside, shouting, and she wondered if he was annoying Hugh or if Hugh was teasing him. There was a scream. Perhaps the teasing had gone too far and they were fighting seriously now. 'Listen,' she said. 'Listen to that boy. I wonder what he's up to now. I'll bet my bottom dollar he hasn't got that water yet. I've been telling him about it ever since we got up.'

'You worry too much,' Rixon said.

[9]

'So you say. But I'm the one who'll be stuck with him if this weather lasts. Listen to that wind.'

'It's only an East wind,' Rixon said, dismissing it. 'It won't do any harm.' He put down his shoes and pulled on his wellington boots. 'In another two years all your problems will be over, Dell. As soon as I shake the dust of the bank off my feet for the last time, your life will be a bed of roses. I'll do all the work and you can stay in bed till lunchtime every day.' He had reached the door and he was looking out at the two boys as they loaded Hugh's books into the Fiat.

'When you retire, Tom, let's go away somewhere. We always said we'd travel when we had the time. We haven't had a holiday for years.'

Rixon turned down his socks over the rims of his boots. 'I don't see the point of holidays. Beaches, museums, mosquitoes. Anyway all our money's tied up here.' When he bent down a slight vein reddened in his face. 'Unless, of course, we win the pools. Or unless I rob the bank.' He looked up at her and smiled. 'Or better still, you go and have a holiday with old Robinette. You're still the apple of his eye. He's always asking you to go back. Gladden an old man's heart, just like he says. Then when he leaves you all his money in his will, you can travel the world to your heart's content.'

She looked away from the real Rixon to the old photograph of him on the mantelpiece. 'I've told you before, I don't like that kind of talk.'

'A joke, that's all.'

'It's not my idea of a joke.'

Since the picture on the mantelpiece had been taken Rixon had changed in many ways. His hair had gone grey, he had that stoop which she had begun to notice recently and now, she decided, something inside him had changed too.

'The old man's invitations are to both of us—' she said.

Rixon stood at the door and stamped his feet down into his wellington boots and she saw that he was looking out at the land, watching the snow settling on the acres which he owned. 'Being able to spend all my time farming this place: that will be enough holiday for me.'

Della slipped her stockinged feet into her own wellington boots. 'And that,' she said, 'is precisely what I thought you'd say.'

The boy twisted a finger in his awkward hair. 'I wish I hadn't mended your rotten old car. You'd have had to stay here then. I could have pinched the distributor. I could have pinched the whole car if I'd wanted to.'

'And hidden it away?'

Hugh modelled the body of a miniature snowman on the Fiat.

The boy's eyes searched the desolate landscape for a hiding place.

'I wish you would stay,' Della said. 'I'm afraid that if there's any more snow, you might get stranded in a ditch somewhere.'

'Whizzee, whizzee,' the boy circled the car, shouting. 'You'll skid into the gutter like them cops. Bzz, bzz, bzz, them cops chasing that fellow on that road.' He stopped suddenly and his big, destructive hand crept towards Hugh's snowman.

Della, watching, began to feel the cold biting into her flesh and she wondered why it was that some people welcomed snow. She looked beyond the boys. As a child she had always hated it; she had hated snowballs, snowmen, sledges, skis. The snow fell in straight piercing lines, making a barrier between her and the car.

'If you touch that snowman—' Hugh told the boy.

It would be nice to be warm, she thought, living in some comfortable clime.

'I need a bit of help here, Dell,' Rixon called from behind her. 'I need help with this bull.'

Whichever way she turned she was stung by the blinding lines of the snow. 'Not on your life,' she said. 'I told you that if you were fool enough to buy that bull, you'd have to do everything for it yourself. I'm not risking getting trampled underfoot. I'm having nothing to do with it. In any case, I'm helping Hugh. I want him to get on his way before the weather gets any worse.'

'This kind of snow never settles,' Rixon said. 'The wind's in the wrong direction anyway.'

Della kicked at a mound of snow which had already settled.

'A conflict situation?' Hugh said. 'Father says Go and Mother says Stop. Dan, you have the casting vote.' He turned to the boy and clasped his hand in a trial of strength. They both gritted their teeth, ready for the contest, and they rested their elbows on the Fiat. It was a feat they had observed in the many westerns they had watched.

'Stop that,' Della said. 'One of you will be getting hurt.' She watched the little snowman perish in the strife.

The boy shrieked out: 'I'll break his bloody fingers off and he can't drive with no fingers on.'

'It'd take a better man than you.'

'Stop it,' Della called out again.

Hugh's fingers alternating with the boy's were delicate. She looked at the ten fingers, counting them: Hugh's, Daniel's, Hugh's, Daniel's, Hugh's. The boy's rough fingers with their dirty nails might crush those of her son. She started toward them, forgetting that the idea of touching the boy was as repugnant to her as the idea of touching Rixon's bull.

'I'll break your bloody arm off, Hugh.'

She was near to them now and she saw that the boy's fingers were bending back and then she saw him giving in. The cold snow stung her.

The boy massaged his fingers. 'You,' she said. 'You'd better find something more useful to do. I'll go and get the rest of Hugh's things, he won't be staying now.'

The phrase: 'If Eugene had lived' came back into her mind again.

Rixon stroked the bull's head roughly with his fist.

'I wish you'd leave that slobbering beast alone, Tom.'

'Della nourishes a secret passion for you, Pride. She pretends to find you repulsive, but deep down she's like What's-'er-name in Greek mythology.'

[12]

'What is her name?'

'I forget. Pity Hugh's gone. He would have known. His mind is full of bits of information like that. Who was it? All I remember is that she used to garland the bull's neck with flowers.'

Della looked at the terrible folding of flesh around the bull's neck. 'It must have been a different kind of bull.'

Rixon fed it a handful of hay. 'There isn't anything wrong with Pride. Our trouble is the bureaucrats and all that fuss over the milk licence.'

The bull moved towards him.

'Watch out,' Della said. 'I wish you'd take more care. Look at that wild look in its eyes.'

'Nonsense. He's as gentle as a kitten.'

'If we'd wanted a kitten—'

'I know, I know. We could have spoken to the cat.'

The bull made one of its groaning noises. Della wiped moisture from her face. In the bull's shed she felt hot, as if she might be feverish. What am I doing here? she asked herself. If Eugene had lived I'd never have set foot inside a barn. I doubt if I'd have known that places like this exist. She glanced at Rixon. He did not seem handsome today, today was one of his tired days. She recalled that he had slept poorly the night before.

'You're feeling all right, aren't you, Tom?'

'Don't I look all right?'

'You're overdoing things; the bank, this place.'

She saw him straighten up. 'This place is no problem, not to me.'

'Why *don't* we take a holiday?'

'I don't need a holiday.'

I should have stayed on with the old man, she thought. I could have had a sane, sensible, civilized life. The bull stared at a point beyond her.

'The energy you spend on that bull is ridiculous,' she said. 'We'll have to get rid of it. You know that as well as I do.'

A picture of the Robinette house in Mimosa Street came into her mind. She would like to be there now with Eugene and with the old man, maybe with the brood of children the old man said they ought to have had. She would have been waited on by the black cook, driven about by the black chauffeur. She would have done the *New York Times* crossword every Sunday to sharpen up her wits in case they softened in the summer heat. She would have ridden the high speed lift up to Robinette's office suite, which would have been Eugene's by now. She would have vacationed at luxury hotels, sailed on the old man's yacht—

'If we sell it now whilst it's young,' she said, insisting, 'we can recoup our money.' Eugene's money, if you wanted to be precise. She passed a bucket over to Rixon so that he could top up the water in the trough, breaking her rule by helping him to tend the bull.

He smiled at her. 'I think you're a little bit jealous of poor old Pride. Strange things, bulls. So powerful. You can see why they're obsessed by them in Spain. They call out to something primitive in you.'

And for this, Della thought, I have thrown in my widow's mite. 'The primitive urge to kill,' she said.

The smell of the bull seemed to invade the house.

She tried to remember who the maiden in mythology was who had been carried away by the bull. There was an old copy of *Peter Parley's Tales* somewhere about the house: she might find some reference in there. She looked at herself in the mirror over the mantelpiece. She had got into the habit of studying her face out of curiosity, to see what changes the wind and weather were wreaking in it. If Eugene had lived there would have been no farm, she assured her reflection in the mirror. No farm, no toil, no boy, no bull. And there's more truth in that than meets the eye. If Eugene had not encountered that shell there would have been no legacy, no money to buy this farm, this wilderness which Rixon had always craved. Without the money they could never have bought these wasted acres, the animals, the little Fiat which she had given to Hugh. No money to pay for Hugh's expensive education, his books, his records, his aesthetic tastes. She looked straight into the mirror, but she did not seem to see the face that filled it. She seemed to be searching for another face. If I were still married to you, Eugene, things would have been different. And, if you had to go and die, what in hell's name did you leave me that money for? You bought me into this drudgery, do you realize that? For Christ's sake, do you know what you've done? You've fulfilled Tom's dream but, Goddamn it, you've shattered mine!

She heard the boy's voice behind her: 'Missus, old Rixon's gone. Are you talking to me?'

She swung around on him: 'I've told you before, you're not to creep about like that. I don't know how you do it with those big feet of yours. You seem to enjoy scaring people.' She tied a scarf around her neck and searched for some dry gloves. 'Now for God's sake, get ready and let's go. We'd better get all the work done before the weather gets any worse or we'll be in trouble. Just you wait and see.'

'You don't like living here, do you, Missus?' the boy asked as they carried water to the cows.

'Why do you say that?'

He had not put his gloves on and his hands were blue with cold. If only he would be sensible, wear proper clothes, leave the snow alone. He swung the buckets as he carried them and the water spilt out, leaving a clear trail in the snow. Della did not tell him to stop doing this because it might be that he swung his arms in an effort to keep his circulation going. Besides she had decided that *some* water was better than no water.

'Old Rixon says you hate this place.'

'Watch what you're doing; there won't be any water left.' She drew the wooden peg out of the cowshed door. There were six cows in this building and they were, in her opinion, in too close proximity to each other.

'Is it true what old Rixon said?'

'Most of the things on this farm could do with a little more comfort, including me.'

The crippled cow leaned its heavy body against the wooden pen so that it could get at the water. Della spoke to it with something in her voice which she never used to the animals when Rixon was around. The cow looked at her, responding to her tone.

'My Uncle Charlie says that cow ought to be put to sleep.'

'That's a coincidence, I've always thought your Uncle Charlie should be put to sleep.'

The boy scrutinized the lame cow very closely. 'My Uncle Charlie says it's cruel the way you and old Rixon let it suffer. He says its leg will get worse and worse and worse.'

'I'll be darned, I didn't know your Uncle Charlie was a vet.'

'He works for a plumber, Missus, you know that.'

'What a waste. He could go far in the animal world.'

'He keeps pigeons.'

'What better training ground.' There was a small sore place on the cow's head and she touched the area around it lightly. 'And if you're so concerned about the welfare of the animals all of a sudden, you can try doing a bit of work for a change. See that they're fed and given water, for example.'

The boy pondered this, keeping silent as he did whenever a new idea was presented to him. His mouth moved as he chewed it over. Then the mouth movements stopped as if he were about to answer back. He bent down to pick up a bucket and slowly emptied its contents into one of the troughs. Della looked at his face: she wished she had not said what she had said about his Uncle Charlie and she tried to think of something else to say, something lighter. He had begun to swing the empty bucket, letting it bang against the bars of the pen.

'Don't do that, Daniel,' she said and she made herself touch his sleeve to restrain him. 'Your uncle isn't on his own, you know. There are a lot of people who think they know all there is to know about animals. They don't understand that you've either got to be born to farm life or you've got to go somewhere and study it properly. Mr Rixon's a little bit like your uncle. He loves animals, of course, particularly that bull, but in other ways he's got no idea at all. I'm always telling him that if you want animals to thrive, you've got to give them attention. They're not like weeds. Cows need cowmen; sheep need shepherds.' She looked at him. 'You understand what I'm saying, don't you? Mr Rixon is crazy about this farm: he's wanted it ever since he was a boy. It's just that he doesn't begin to understand animals.' She watched the expression on the boy's face. 'Sometimes I wonder why I waste my breath trying to carry on conversations with you.' He shook his head up and down and then from side to side. 'I don't suppose what I'm saying is of any interest to you. Why should it be?' The boy opened his eyes very wide, trying to look as if he was following her words. 'It's no use buying a farm like this and then going off to the bank every day and leaving someone else to take care of it.'

'You and me?'

'Yes, you and me. It's not our farm, is it?'

The boy's eyes were keen and crooked: 'Palming all the work off on to you and me.'

Often the boy awakened in her a kind of wariness. It began somewhere in her chest like the pain she had felt sometimes recently. 'I didn't say that. Mr Rixon works very, very hard. He has an important job. It's not easy being a bank manager.' It's not like being a plumber, she would have liked to say.

The boy was swinging the bucket again. 'My Uncle Charlie says old Rixon doesn't know a pig from an elephant.' She ignored his laugh. 'You know what he calls this place? He calls it "Rixon's Folly".'

'What a talented man your Uncle Charlie is. He ought to be writing comedy shows for television. Why does he squander all his repartee in the drains of Manchester?' She made herself go on with her work. She had fallen into another of the boy's traps: 'Old Rixon can't tell a tractor from a wheelbarrow,' he'd tell his uncle. 'The Missus told me so herself.'

The boy blew on his cold hands.

She began to feel angry. She was angry with herself for her indiscretion, angry with Rixon for planting her at this farm, angry with Eugene for dying. Rixon would be drinking his hot milky coffee now. He would be smiling, listening, advising: 'The hottest tip on the market, Madam. Come and buy.' Rixon's Folly. White Elephant Farm. Why did he always take on things no one else would tolerate: the farm, the bull, the boy?

She patted the lame cow on its side and then she said to the boy: 'Come on. We'll have to fill all the buckets again. Whatever we do, we mustn't run out of water. Then we'll have some coffee, made with milk, like the girls make for Mr Rixon at the bank and, after that, we'll bring the sheep down from the moor field.'

'Old Rixon said we was to leave those woolly bastards up there where they are.'

'Stop saying that.' She stacked the buckets.

' "Woolly bastard"?'

'And stop saying "Old Rixon" too.'

'The lads down at the billiard room call him "Old Rixon".'

'I don't want to know.'

'He said we had to leave them woolly bastards up there.'

'I don't care what he said.'

'He'll go mad.'

'He can tear the farm down once this snow goes. It's *now* I'm worrying about.'

The boy smiled; his mouth widened and his eyes became slits. Then he began to move quickly; he slotted his arms through the handles of the buckets, carrying his own and Della's too. He went outside. Although the snow ravaged his face he turned it upwards, letting flakes of snow settle on his nose. Della, following him, found herself looking at the menacing sky from which violent streaks of snow came down. She shivered and asked herself for the millionth time what insanity had led her to invest Eugene's money in this crazy place.

The boy had reached the tap. He turned three circles, swinging the buckets round and round. 'Stand still,' she screamed

[18]

at him. He grinned at her and then he shuffled his feet in the steps of some kind of a dance. Then he set the buckets down and, struggling with the stiff tap, began to fill them up with water. A wind was getting up and she could not be sure that it was the benign East wind of which her husband had spoken. The boy, with the full buckets in his hands, was spinning around again.

'You half-wit.'

The storm had brought out the demon in him, the demon which the magistrate had said must be subdued, the demon which made him steal cars and tear the cables out of telephone kiosks. The slight pain which sometimes invaded Della's side struck at her. Let him dance, she thought. There'll be enough time for him to watch his step when his dancing days are done, like mine.

She had not intended to look in on the bull again, but it was making more noise than the boy. She opened the door just enough to see inside. The bull was massive, black and blundering. Its dehorned head looked too small for its gross black body. It lurched, not seeing her. She stood back. Rixon had not secured it properly, as he had promised always to do. He doesn't give a fig for me, she thought. It could crush me to pulp for all he cares. The bull turned towards her and she was reminded of a sea animal. A whale: clumsy, floundering because it had left the ocean. Its slanting, unfathomable navy blue eyes looked past her. She spoke out loud to it, something she had never done before: 'You foul, black mass. You're the worst thing about this ugly farm.' The bull slurped its water in the trough. The folds of its flesh shook. She looked for a long time at its thick body. The animal approached her. She felt for the penknife which she always kept in her pocket, a scout knife abandoned long ago by Hugh. Her thumb-nail worked at the clasp. 'Come any nearer and I'll slaughter you.' Her teeth were gritted and she knew that she would enjoy the sight of the bull's black blood. 'For God's sake,' she stopped herself. 'This place is driving you clean out of your mind.' She let the blade of the knife spring back into place and she backed away from the bull. 'The way I'm going on, they'll be taking me away.' She fastened the door and went outside and looked out at the sparse horizon. Some earlier occupants of the farm had cut down nearly all the trees. She hunched her shoulders, thinking of the shelter from the cold they might have brought. 'Spilt milk, like everything else,' she told herself.

The postman was already inside the house, warming his fleshy hands before the fire. He sat on the edge of the chair, his fat body tipping it towards the hearth. She pulled off her wellingtons at the door and left them on the step. The postman gestured, welcoming her.

'Nasty morning,' he said. 'I was telling the lad, it's a long time since I saw weather like this up here.' They both looked around for the boy. 'I was telling him, it's like it was in nineteen forty when them poor Thompsons got snowed in up here.' He banged his hands together. 'I've told you about me and them Varley's lads digging them out, haven't I?'

'Frequently. You told me at the first sign of a snowflake last winter.'

'Well, you know all about it then.' He reached his arm out toward the cat, trying to touch it, to establish contact with it. 'I saw your husband just now, on his way into town. He's not going to be on time today, not with the roads the way they are. There's a fair bit of black ice down near the bridge, there'll be a few cars come off the roads. He'll have a good excuse for being late. Mind you, he's lucky to get away from this place.' The postman gave up the struggle to reach the cat and banged his hands together again. 'I had a hard time getting up this road.

It's the worst place for miles around when you get bad weather. Always has been. But I thought: I can't let Mrs Rixon down. I know she likes to get her letters. I don't know what you'd do without those white and blue envelopes.' The banging of his hands continued. 'Can't think what he finds to write about, that friend of yours.'

'My father-in-law,' Della said. 'My first husband's father.'

Still the banging of the hands and then the postman blew and groaned. Signals, Della thought. Food, drink.

'Coffee?' she said. 'I gather you've been struck by the cold.'

'I wouldn't say no.' He looked at her with his small eyes. Unlike the boy's, his gaze was straight. 'Your husband was telling me that your Hugh was going back to Cambridge today. I wouldn't fancy driving there, not on a day like this.' Hugh's body, mangled, his blood staining his fine hair, lay on the motorway, freezing in the ice: the thought caused her own eyes to enlarge.

'He's an expert driver.'

'That's right, they say when he leaves this place, he drives like a bat let out of hell.'

She passed him to go into the kitchen.

'Tea's all right if it's easier,' the postman said.

'It isn't.' She snatched at the tin of coffee.

'This snow,' the postman said. 'It's setting in. Listen to that wind. It's a bad sign when you get a wind like that. That wind comes from the moors.' The wind did howl now, so that from the kitchen it was not easy to hear the postman's words. She held on to the kettle lid, helping it to boil.

'It's only an East wind,' she said, having no idea what that signified.

'East wind? Never. It comes from over there.' She could not see which way his hand pointed from where she was. 'When the wind whistles like that, there's trouble on the way.'

'Next you'll tell me that that's the very wind the poor Thompsons heard before they died.' She waited.

'Them poor Thompsons—'

'On such a morn as this?'

The kettle boiled and the sound of the steam mingled with the sound of the wind so that she had difficulty catching on to what the postman said about the Thompsons. 'Coughing', 'sneezing', 'snapping bones', 'frozen in the chair', 'hanging by his neck'. She poured boiling water into the cups. She remembered that she had told the boy that he could have his coffee made with milk. She wondered where he was and why he always hid away when the postman came.

'No wonder they say this place is haunted, Mrs Rixon. Both of them dead as doornails when we dug them out.'

'The only people who say this place is haunted say it because they hope they'll frighten us into selling it at a very low price. I've never seen any ghosts or heard them either.' Unless you counted the ghost of Eugene, that was.

'They say poor old Thompson has been seen roaming about this place with the rope still round his neck.'

'And *Mrs* Thompson in her brown paper and vinegar liberty bodice?'

The postman reached out for his coffee. 'I'm not one for believing in ghosts. I'm only telling you what people say.' When he drank, he slurped like the bull. He spooned more sugar into his cup.

'There are some biscuits,' Della said. 'Help yourself, before the Thompsons get them. I'd better go and look for the boy.' The postman dipped two ginger biscuits into his coffee. She reached the door and called out: 'Daniel!'

'Daniel!' the postman echoed after her. 'Come on, come in. Do as the Missus tells you.' He eased his position, sitting back in Rixon's chair so that all four of its legs were firmly on the ground. 'They say in the village you've been a right good 'un to that rascal there. They say not many would have taken him on.'

'I can't think why anyone should say that.' But a voice inside her agreed: I've been a bloody martyr, if they really want to call me names.

'That lad has dropped into a cosy billet.' He drank down the last sugary dregs of coffee. 'Yes, it's a real cosy billet. You've got some nice pieces here.' He looked around the room.

'He has the same conditions as any employee would.'

'They say you and Mr Rixon treat him as if he were your own. I'll bet my bottom dollar, he's never been in a place like this before.'

'This place? He lived,' she stirred her coffee loudly, 'in a suburb in Manchester with his aunt and uncle. No doubt if you ever get round to handing out the mail, there'll be a letter from his Auntie Millie, lavender envelopes. They have a semi in Didsbury, very nice. They enjoy many small luxuries denied to me: fitted carpets, a brand new three piece (uncut moquette), a cocktail cabinet, white melamine (and believe me, Auntie Millie's white *is* white), a two-door fridge, a colour television and pelmets with gold tassels on. I do hope you'll report all this. I like to keep the records straight!'

'Gold tassels, eh?'

'I forgot the goldfish tank. Encrusted with artificial seaweed, very picturesque. They have several goldfish which have grown as big as trout, possibly it's something to do with the daylight lighting. They have strips of that in every room. Auntie Millie says it makes her feel as if she lives outside, which, as she never actually goes outside, is probably a necessary experience. When they're not watching the colour television, they sit and watch the goldfish opening and closing their little mouths. So, I assure you, Daniel is used to more comfort there than he'll ever get here.'

'I don't suppose it's much cop watching goldfish for a lad, even if they are as big as trout.'

Della walked past him again and called out once more. 'I doubt if he's even got his jersey on,' she said.

'When I got here I said: ' "You want to get your coat on before you catch your death." ' '

She could see the boy now, outside the door, hands in the pockets of his jeans; he was kicking at a snow-covered log. His wild hair was wet and he wore no hat. He kept his head down as if that were an excuse for not hearing Della's call.

[23]

'Well, people always have a lot to say,' the postman said. 'I keep telling them. They go on about him being on probation.'

'He isn't on probation.'

'I tell them that. He doesn't look as if he'd have the gumption to steal a car. Anybody can twist a few wires out of a telephone box, but taking a car is different.' He looked deep into his empty cup. 'Not enough gumption. Comes down to the billiard room, stands about looking at his feet. Never bothers anyone, but he's not quite plumb in the middle. Not a hundred per cent that lad.'

'There's nothing wrong with Daniel'.

'Nothing wrong? They say he can't even read and write. A boy of his age and he can't read and write. They say you took something on and no mistake. It's to your credit though, that's what I say.'

She opened the door wide so that the cold wind which the postman insisted did not come from the East might invade the house and drive him out of it. She went over to the boy and spoke to him: 'Come in, when I call you. I've made some coffee for you and it's getting cold. I've told you not to go out without your anorak.'

'I'm filling up the buckets like you said.'

'We filled the buckets before. So come on in.' The boy gave her his slanted look. 'I'll bring your coffee, you'd better drink it in the garage; you'll catch pneumonia standing out here in this snow.' She shrugged her shoulders and went into the house.

'Won't he come in then?' the postman asked. 'Taking his coffee out to him? You'll make him too soft the way you run around.'

'Mr Marsden,' Della asked, 'was this some kind of a social call? Did you drive up here in the snow to inquire about our state of health or was there by any chance some mail for us? Bills? Postcards? Reminders from the Inland Revenue?' She took his cup from him, not offering to refill it. 'Because if there isn't any mail, I still have work to do.'

'I'll say this, Missus. Your husband is a lucky man. The way

[24]

he goes off and leaves all the work to you. They say you've helped him over many a stile. They say you're the one who always bails him out.' He patted the pockets of the donkey jacket which Della had not invited him to remove. 'I must be losing my memory, I've left your letters outside in the van. I'll go and get them if the van's still there. I hope that lad's not gone joy-riding in it.'

She stood by the door as he went out. 'It must be hard for you to remember the letters, when you've so many other things on your mind.'

'There's one for your Hugh. Pity he went off early. I could have given it to him. Looks as if it's from some girl.' He took a bundle of letters from the van and began to sort them out slowly, reluctant to hand them over. 'Yes, there's that purple one for the lad, from his Auntie Millie in Manchester, is it? And two, no three, of them white and blue ones for you.' The blue-winged envelopes were captured in his hands; snow fell on the Western Union sign. 'And here's that one I told you about for your Hugh. Look here, it says "Hugh Rixon". They never say "Mr" now, it's not the modern way. He's had a lot of letters with that writing on.' He put the letter into her hands, exposing the blue ink to the snow. 'If you want to write his address on, I can take it and post it on to him.' The postman's eyebrows were thick and ugly, solid snow-laden shelves of hair.

'No, I'll send it on later in the day. I can open it and telephone it on tonight if the message is important.'

'He won't like that. They don't like their mothers looking at their letters. You'd better let me take it, looks like *you* might be getting snowed in.'

'My husband says the wind is blowing in the wrong direction.'

'Makes me laugh, talking as if he was bred up here. But I hope he's right. I keep thinking of them poor Thompsons, it started just like this. And you know how they ended up. Stone dead.'

Della's next sentence was lost in the whistling wind.

'There are worse fates than that,' was what she said.

[25]

'Hugh's been waiting for a letter,' the boy said. 'He's been waiting for old Marsden every day.'

'He didn't wait today.' She handed him his own letter. 'And wash your grimy hands before you open that. Your Auntie Millie wouldn't like it if you got finger marks on her nice clean lavender envelopes. Has she got lavender sheets and pillow cases and towels and cakes of soap?'

'I don't know what lavender means, Missus.' He poked a finger or two under a thin stream of water from the tap and then he wiped his fingers on the oven cloth.

'Not on that! When will you ever learn?'

He slipped the envelope into the torn pocket of his jeans, unopened and unread. She wanted to offer to read it for him, but she did not do so. If he felt curious about Auntie Millie's message then he must ask. She decided that she would open the Western Union envelopes now, though she already knew their contents; they had already been telephoned by the Western Union Man: NEW ICE AGE APPROACHES STOP EXTRA PRE-CAUTION AGAINST WINTER ILLS STOP DOSAGES OF GAMMA GLOBULIN DESPATCHED STOP ADMINSTER SELF STOP RIXON STOP SON GLUTEUS MAXIMUS STOP.

Shouldn't the plural be 'maximi'? Her mind calculated how many of them there were in the family. Two: Rixon; two: herself; two: Hugh. (Four, if he had secretly married the writer of the blue-inked envelopes.) PLEASE INCREASE ALL DOSAGES BY TWENTY-FIVE PER CENT, she might cable back, or should it be by thirty per cent? She sighed at the arithmetic.

'You get these envelopes every day. Why do you get them every day?'

'Not on Sundays.'

'Every other day—'

'An old man I used to know. He worries about my health.'

She felt suddenly very tired, as if one of the infections the old man dreamed up had attacked her.

CARIBBEAN STILL REPRESENTS A HAVEN STOP JOIN ME WIPE OUT WINTER ILLS.

The thought of the Caribbean warmed her. Even in these days there must be luxury there for tourists. Yachts, luxury hotels, the deep blue sea.

'Why does that old man worry about *your* health?'

'Because we're related. Or we used to be. He was my father-in-law once, my first husband's father. I suppose he got into the habit of worrying about it then.' She tried to think of the location of the Caribbean on the globe and of the political climate there. There had been some trouble recently, where was it?

'Fancy you having two husbands, Missus.'

'I haven't got two husbands.'

'I mean that Eugene.'

'Daniel, Eugene died a long time ago, you know that very well. I told you the other day, he died in the Korean War.' But however often she said it, it was something she still found hard to believe herself. It was something never quite accepted. Eugene had never really died; he had stayed there alive somewhere in her mind. Sometimes he seemed more alive to her than Rixon.

'Hugh said you're always thinking about that old Eugene.'

'Don't be silly. Hugh couldn't have said that to you. You make things up.' She went to the door. 'Get your things. We've wasted enough time talking, it's time we went and got the sheep.'

'Woolly bastards,' the boy said. 'I don't want to go up there.' He prodded at the cat with the bent toe of his stockinged feet.

'No, *I* don't want to go up there either. I'd like to sit by the fire and write letters or read a book, but there are things we have to do whether we like it or not. Believe me, there are lots of things I'd rather do.' Catch up on the Sunday papers, do my knitting. Fly off to the Caribbean, leave all of you behind. I'd like to be at Kennedy Airport, La Guardia then, meeting Eugene

[27]

back from one of his trips. If only he had lived— The outside looked cold. 'Come on,' she said, 'get ready. I want them down here before there's much more snow.'

She folded up the two cables she had just read and turned to the third: BESEECH YOU STOP RETURN AND GLADDEN AN OLD MAN'S HEART STOP. She smiled at the quality of the prose. SUCCOUR ESSENTIAL IN THE DECLINING YEARS.

'I don't know what you're laughing at, Missus.'

She held the cable up and moved it in front of his eyes. 'Well, you'll just have to learn to read if you want to share that joke, won't you?' she said.

⊱❈⊰

The dogs, jubilant to be released from the buildings where they lived, barked and scampered into the face of the snow. Della and the boy walked in single file down the drive and up to the moor edge. Della walked carefully, watching her feet, fearing that she might trip and fall over one of the large stones which had come off the drystone wall and which had never been replaced by Rixon. She feared that she might twist an ankle or even break a leg like poor Mrs Thompson. The track was dry and rough, the pools in the uneven earth were freezing over and beginning to be covered by a layer of snow. The boy went on ahead, his gangling body swaying in one of his weird dances, his long legs bent at the knees and his large feet spread out in wide bizarre steps. For a time she tried to follow in his footsteps, but her own gait became erratic. His stride was too long, too wide. His breath hit the icy air like smoke. 'Them horses, Missus,' he called suddenly. 'They're not moving. Looks as if they're dead.'

She stopped, watching them, almost putting out a hand as if to call them to her for food, but they stayed still as if they had been turned to stone.

The boy danced on in front of her. 'It's coming down thicker,' he shouted. 'I'll make myself a snowman if it lasts.' She shivered and turned towards the moors. It *was* thicker there. She began to wonder if the postman had been right. Would it get worse? She tried to recall the snatches of history she had heard about the Thompsons and that other snow. That terrible story about the two of them being found dead, one in the house and one in the outbuildings. But, for God's sake, that was thirty years ago; there were telephones now, snow-ploughs, helicopters, aeroplanes. So what are you worrying about? she asked herself. There's no chance of being trapped at this hateful farm, not in this day and age.

'Why don't you like this farm?' the boy asked, as if he could read her thoughts. He stooped to pick up a large tree root. 'Old Rixon says you want a semi like my Auntie Millie's got. But he says you'll have to live in it on your own because he's never leaving here.' She stumbled. The near fall jarred her more severely than a real fall would have done. She looked out at the snow-bound moors; there was no dividing line between the white sky and the white earth. She knew that through the curtain of snow there was nothing but a waste land. How many miles of it? Fifty? Seventy?

'Why don't you like this farm?'

With her cold breath she said: 'You're always asking me that.'

'Where would you like?' the boy persisted, but he did not wait for her to answer. 'I'll tell you what I like. I like towns. I like Manchester. I like London, Birmingham. I like America where you get them telegrams from.'

'America is not a town.' But there was no point arguing on such a day.

He flung the tree root for the dogs and she watched them tearing after it. 'I don't care where it is. As soon as I've saved up, I'm off.'

She pulled up the hood of her anorak for warmth. The snow bit at her uncovered face.

'Yes, I'm off. A million bloody miles from here.'

Ah well, why not? Somewhere over those bleak moors there were railways, bus stations, art galleries, life. She thought of

Hugh travelling to Cambridge and she thought how she would like to visit him, take tea in the college, listen to Hugh's views. She would be like those other mothers who did not have to work on crazy farms.

'Like that lad on television, he stowed away on a big boat, got off in America and bought himself a big car. Zoom, zoom, zoom!' He swerved too close to her and she pushed at him.

'The penitentiary is all you'll see of America unless you mend your ways.' She must not think of Cambridge any more. Hugh had outgrown her. In future she must base her fantasies elsewhere.

'Did you have a big one when you were in America?'

'Big what?'

'Big car?'

'I didn't have a car at all. Eugene was teaching me to drive, but then—'

'You lived in America and you didn't even have a rotten car.' He darted ahead of her and threw a twig for the dogs. They ran off, dashing up the snow. She looked back at the road from the farm to the village. Eugene's Lincoln would have been too large for that road. Too wide. In fact, if more snow piled up, no car would make it up that road. What then? A carless world and a boy with fourteen car thefts to his name. She tried to quicken her pace to catch up with him. He had reached the moorland paddock now and she saw him leap the small stream near the stone wall. The dogs chased after him, barking, frenzied.

'For God's sake, idiot. Calm those dogs down. Here boys, here.'

The boy sat on the wall, waiting; he kicked his heels against the stone. 'What do you want me to do now?' he asked.

'To begin with, get off that wall. It's covered with snow.'

'Don't know why we're bothering with these woolly bastards,' he said.

'Don't start all that again.'

'Old Rixon said he didn't want them moving.'

'And stop calling him that. You're getting too big for your boots.'

[30]

The dogs and sheep stood quietly, waiting for a word. The animals looked surprisingly alike, their pointed faces listening. She had never thought that sheep were stupid and in this snow their faces looked bright like those of the dogs. She noted the elegance of their delicate black legs.

'Come on,' she said.

'Mr Rixon said we was to leave them here.'

'From now on you'll take your orders from me.'

'It isn't your farm.'

'That's all you know. It was bought with *my* money.' My legacy from Eugene. 'Three-quarters of it is mine, maybe more. So just get off that wall, run round there and take the dogs with you. I'll stand here and guide the sheep on to the lane.'

His long legs swung off the wall as slowly as he dared. The dogs ran hither and thither, confused by him.

The last straw, Della decided. The Social Services can find another pair of idiots to take him on. The sheep began, at last, to filter from the field. She patted one of the dogs. 'Thank God,' she said, 'something on this farm has a brain.'

The boy followed the animals from the field, leaving Della to fasten the gate. He walked in front of her. His crooked path had been erased by the new falling snow; the track he made now was straight and regular.

'I've made up my mind this time,' she said. 'You'll have to pack your traps and go.' He walked on, still in front, not seeming to heed what she said. He stopped once to pick up a stick, shook the snow from it and swished it from side to side. 'There must be some normal boys who want to work on farms.' The boy began to run. The dogs ran too, barking at his heels. The sheep quickened their pace so that she feared for their black legs. She became afraid that he would encourage the dogs to drive the sheep too far, into danger, on to the road. She went behind them as quickly as she could, along the path, along the lane. 'You needn't stop to pack your things, I'll send them after you.'

At the end of the lane she saw that he had herded all the sheep into the bottom field. He had secured the gate and he was leaning on the fence. The dogs played at his feet.

She put her hand to the place where the pain in her chest had been.

'What the hell do you think you're doing?'

'What you told me, Missus. Settling them woolly bastards in.'

She gasped for breath in the cold air. He looked at her, his head inclining to one side, a way of looking at her which always made her angry.

'I always do what you tell me, Missus.'

It was still very early in the day, but she felt as tired as if she had been at work for many hours. It was hard to believe that for many people the snow-filled day had just begun.

❖❖❖

The telephone was ringing as they got back to the house. The boy quickened his pace to answer it. She had forgotten that telephones were one of his passions.

'Yep,' she heard him say and she saw him look through the pages of the directory as if to confirm a number, moving his head from side to side exactly as if he could read. He had even adopted her manner of picking up a pencil simultaneously with the telephone. She took the receiver, frowning at him. For a moment she had difficulty identifying the voice.

'Don't tell me you don't know me.'

'At the moment, I'm afraid I don't.'

'You mean you've forgotten me, after all the messages I've brought you from over there?'

'Western Union. Now I know. But usually you announce yourself.'

The boy stood close to her, trying to hear both ends of the conversation. She jerked her elbow, telling him to go away.

'I did announce myself.'

'Yes, the boy got to the phone first.'

[32]

'In any case, I thought you knew my voice by now.'

'I did know it. But you've been away. There was another man last week. Have you been ill?'

'Flu. I'm still feeling weak.'

'Maybe you should rest your voice.'

'Can't desert my post. There are two today so far. They came almost simultaneously.'

'A cure for slight chest pains, I hope.'

'Not this time. I'm having difficulty deciding which to read first.'

'Does it matter?'

'I take pride in my work, I like to get the sequence right.'

'Just a minute.' She signalled to the boy with her free hand. 'Will you go away?'

'Me?' the Western Union Man said.

'Him.' The boy stood his ground.

'Suggest he goes out. There's many an untended Rolls abandoned in the snow.'

'He's happier in here torturing me.'

The Western Union Man sighed. 'Well, I'll begin.' He cleared his throat. 'This is a very interesting one: MIRACLE CURE EVOLVED FOR DISEASED HAIR STOP. That's funny, you don't sound like someone with diseased hair.'

'Strange you should say that. It's the one thing I haven't got.'

'I've been thinking a lot about your hair. Sometimes when the lines are silent I fall to imagining it, wondering what colour it might be.'

'Imagination is a dangerous thing.'

'Your voice sounds like a flaming redhead's voice.'

'Wrong.'

'A sort of strawberry blonde?'

'Wrong again.'

'I've found it is valuable if I know something about the identity of my clients. If I can form some kind of impression of their physical appearance it seems to help. I've decided, for example, that you're good looking. Am I right?'

'It's as well to keep your illusions intact in this life.' She sat down, worrying because she was not worrying enough about the farm and the work that was still to be done.

'Do you realize,' the Western Union Man said, 'we've spent more time talking to each other than the average man and wife?'

'That's not saying much. Read on.'

'Right: PRESENTLY RESEARCHING STOP WILL COMMUNICATE RESULTS IMMEDIATELY KNOWN.'

'The results of what?'

'The cure for hair.'

'Oh, I'd forgotten that.'

'Now for the second one. Okay? DECISION REGARDING CARIBBEAN REQUIRED URGENTLY STOP COMMUNICATE INTENTIONS PRONTO STOP REPEAT PRONTO. There's a real sense of urgency this time, you get the feeling that your diseased hair can wait, but the Caribbean cannot.'

'Is that all he says?' An image came to her, not of Robinette but of the Western Union Man, sitting under a striped umbrella on a brilliant beach. She visualized the telephone on which he relayed messages as the kind of telephone she had seen used in films about Pacific holidays, slim and light and white. She saw the Western Union Man stirring a long cool drink with a swizzle stick and she wondered what colour the Western Union Man's hair was. Because the Western Union Man always relayed Robinette's words to her, it was hard to picture him as anything but a younger Robinette. Or maybe an older Eugene. 'Do they pay you well for reading cables out to people?' she asked.

'Not as much as I'd like and it may get less. The world of cable senders is contracting. Take your Mr Robinette: if he got tired of sending cables, it'd cause a recession. He's just about our best customer. And he's the only man left in the Western world who can still afford to include the stops.'

'Don't worry, he'll never stop sending cables. They're dyed-in-the-wool with him.'

'And you can guarantee the stops?'

'He always liked precision.'

'I worry sometimes about the medical advice.'

'I never take any of his medicines. They've been following me about for years. My cupboards are full of them.'

'What is he to you? A guardian angel?' The boy had wandered off, he must have heard enough to know that nothing was to be revealed. 'A relation of some kind?'

'A father-figure, I think you'd say. He was my father-in-law for a brief spell.'

'*Was?*'

'You ask a lot of questions, but I can see in your line of business it might help to know. Was. Past tense. My husband died.'

The line had become clouded and she could not hear what the Western Union Man was saying, perhaps he was commiserating with her on her widowhood. Then the line cleared and his voice said: 'There's another message coming in, I suppose I'd better go. I'll post these on?'

'Might as well. The postman also takes a keen interest in my life.' She could not, for the moment, let him go. 'If it helps,' she said, 'I have lightish brown hair. They called it golden when I was a child, but it's got more grey than gold in now. But it's healthy hair. I've always brushed it at least a hundred times a day.'

'Don't worry. I never pay too much attention to what your father-in-law says. And take care of yourself,' the Western Union Man said.

She saw from the window that more snow was falling, much more snow. She turned on the boy: 'And I wish you wouldn't answer that telephone every time it rings, and I wish you wouldn't hover when I'm talking on the phone. There's no privacy when you're around. I don't know why they say the Thompsons haunt this place you're spook enough for me. Anyway, the sheep are all right now. They'll be better in the bottom field whatever Mr Rixon says.'

'He'll go mad when he comes home.'

'Don't be silly.'

'It's *his* farm.'

'Paid for with *my* money. *My* legacy. It took practically all that was left over after I'd educated Hugh. So you can tell your Uncle Charlie to put that in his pipe.' She looked out of the window, down the drive and down the lane towards the road which separated her from Rixon and every inch of it covered with thick snow. 'And another thing; whatever your idol Mr Rixon says, there's a lot more of this weather to come. So if you want to escape from me, you'd better go now. Because if you stay here, you'll be taking a lot of orders from me.' She turned toward him sharply. 'You watch.'

Of course if Eugene had lived there would have been a lot more money, a great deal more. The old man had explained all that to her after Eugene had died.

'All this,' he'd said and he had waved a hand to indicate the house in Mimosa Street. 'This place and the place in Florida—' The apartment in New York, the furniture, the silver, the two hotels, the supermarket chain, the real estate in Alabama, and the half share in the Downtown bank. 'All of it, it was all for my only son. Yes, ma'am. All of it was going to go to him.' It was the only time she ever saw old Robinette like that, with tears splashing down his suntanned face. 'And you won't get a penny of it. No ma'am, you won't get a penny of it to give to some other man.'

Another man.

'You stay here with me. You stay here and be my daughter and then I'll leave it all to you.'

If Eugene had lived. If he had outlived his father— But there was to be no American Dream for her, instead she saw herself turning money over to Rixon. If there had been more money there would have been a bigger, better farm, an endless stretch of barren snow, a more efficient prison for herself. Siberia.

Eugene had not lived. He had died.

[36]

He had inherited nothing from his father.

But all his mother's money had come to her.

'It's your clear bounden duty,' the old man said. 'You took my boy from me; now you've got to take his place.' He talked as if she had sent Eugene to Korea, as if she had been responsible for the planting of the shell. And even now he had not relinquished his hold on her; there was that Caribbean cable to answer. There was only one answer possible, only one logical way to deal with it: No, no, no. But Eugene hadn't taken no for an answer and neither had Rixon, if it came to that. Why should old Robinette? Even if you did have a sense of duty to an obsessed husband and to a son who couldn't get away from you fast enough and to a few animals. She looked to see where the boy was and if he might come into the room, but if he did what did it matter? She found herself picking up the telephone and dialling O. 'Get me Western Union,' she would say. She planned how she would stop saying no. She would send a message to the old man: 'Cable instructions,' it would read. She thought of the words being transmitted at the speed of light. Just let one of those blue-winged envelopes reach the old man and she would be free of this place.

But the operator did not answer. The first link in the chain was faulty. She replaced the receiver, swore softly and dialled O again. She heard a voice, the boy's voice. She started.

'Look at them woolly bastards in that field,' he said. 'They're gonna freeze to death.'

She looked where he pointed at the sheep and at the terrible snow, driving in two directions. There was an East wind, but now there was a West wind too. And then she heard the operator's voice asking her what number she wanted. He asked the number twice.

'Western Union.' Her voice was weak.

'Have you tried their number?'

'No, I didn't realize.'

'Shall I give it to you?'

The sheep were cold and frightened. They stood still like

[37]

victims in the snow. If they had to freeze to death they might be better to do it in familiar surroundings. Perhaps Rixon and the boy were right.

'I have the number here.'

There was a man in some office a long way off, talking to her on the telephone and telling her the number of Western Union so that she could fly away into the sunshine to be a daughter to an old man who had lost his only son in a silly war a long time ago. She should reprimand the man. She should tell him that she was too old to be a daughter to anyone. She was forty-eight, her hair was almost grey, she had arthritis beginning in her legs and sometimes she had a pain in her chest. She had a son of her own, a grown-up man. The man on the telephone ought to be told that when you had a flock of spindly sheep outside your window for whom you were responsible, there was no hope of flight? Didn't he realize they might die of cold before the week was out?

'I'm sorry,' she told the man in her angry voice. 'I don't want the number, it was a mistake.'

'Them woolly bastards,' the boy said and he chuckled to himself.

'Stop saying that,' Della said, slamming the receiver down.

❖❖❖

'Why do you always leave sheep out of your list?'

'Missus?'

'Sheep: you never say that word.'

'Little woolly bastards.' He covered one eye with a hand and he looked at her sideways smiling.

'Why do you always call them that?'

'Don't know what you mean.' He pretended to be listening to his transistor, pressing it tightly to his ear. A voice screamed out that the good times had all gone. The boy's mouth moved to the silent words: 'Good, good, good. Good times gone. You want to

[38]

listen to this, Missus. It's in first place. It's great, isn't it?' She frowned a little, not disagreeing altogether, the man's voice and the tune were pleasing, but what about the sentiments? When she was young they had sung about good times coming, big times, which you were going to share in, they said. But maybe the singer was right, maybe the good times had all gone.

Her good times had all gone and she wondered if there would ever be any good times for the boy.

She got up and went into the kitchen and turned on the tap to fill the kettle.

'Ssh,' the boy said. 'I'm trying to listen to this.'

'Life can't come to a standstill just because you want to listen to those silly songs.' So far there seemed to be no shortage of water. There was no freeze-up yet. The water journeyed into the house from an underground spring, helped on its way by an electric pump they had had fitted two years before. How long would the spring hold out in this weather? The running water drowned out the boy's transistor and she could no longer hear the man telling them that there would be no more good times. She plugged in the kettle and waited for it to boil. She saw in the mirror that the boy was standing behind her, still holding the transistor to his ear so as not to lose any of the sound. His shoulders jigged to the music and Della tapped the handle of the kettle waiting for the steam to rise. The music changed, it became more lively, faster, rapid even, frenzied. There was the backing of a guitar. The kettle boiled and the steam clouded the mirror so that she could no longer see the image of the boy. She put instant coffee into the cups and poured in the water. The boy danced over and helped himself to liberal amounts of sugar, then he beat time to the tune with his spoon. His knees swayed this way and that and his eyes were closed in the kind of ecstasy which young people feel or assume when music plays. Della drank her coffee and decided that she should make more effort to understand the young and their music. She tried to catch on to the tune, humming it between sips. She had put more coal and logs on the fire and the living room was warm; she went in and sat down, moving the cat from the armchair to make room for herself. She closed her mind to the furious storm outside and to all the troubles it might bring. She watched the movements of the boy's long arms and legs, the twisting of his body and the twitching of his nose. And then she remembered that the first time she had ever seen Rixon he had been dancing too. Not dancing on his own as the boy did, but with a lovely, red-haired girl. He was tall like the boy, but he had danced with great style and grace. She had watched him for a very long time, staring at him, just as she was staring at the boy now. The boy had put down the transistor so that his hands were free to clutch at the air. His ungainly arms and legs spread out. But, for some reason, she was not seeing him, she was seeing Rixon all those years ago. She had not felt any jealousy of the girl, she had thought of her and of Rixon as unreal, remote creatures out of her range. She stopped humming and looked at the condensation running down the tiles which she herself had fixed to the wall behind the old oak sideboard; blue, white, blue, white, blue, white. Blue and white tiles, a pattern against which the boy's awkward body spread out with his wild hair, wild face, wild arms and his wild, long fingers grasping at something she could not see. She held on to her coffee cup and she tried to see him as a young girl might, as she had first looked at Rixon. A young girl at a dance, appraising him with his thick unkempt straw-like hair, his big nose flattened to one side, his discoloured twisted teeth, his too big hands and feet. The sole of one of his shoes flapped loose as he trod the air. Her eyes fixed on the forehead and his stupid fringe. The room began to spin a little and she felt dizzy as she had the first time she had seen Rixon at that dance. The damp blue and white tiles dazzled her. The boy's big body swallowed up the air.

She remembered meeting Rixon's eyes over the head of the red-haired girl. She put her coffee cup down: 'Daniel.'

The dance continued.

'Daniel.' Her voice had sharpened.

A knee raised and lowered slowly, his eyes opened and his

arms and legs were stilled, but the music from the transistor still did not stop.

'I've told you before, you're not to dance in here.'

The boy stared at her: his upstretched arms descended slowly. 'Where can I do it then?'

She looked around her, at the snow-crammed windows, at the damp stone walls which Rixon boasted were over two feet thick. She looked at the white ceiling, held up by old oak beams and at the tiles and at the calendar from the seed company, still at December. No one had taken it down, it still hung in the doorway to the kitchen. She stood up and felt unsteady on her feet just as she had done that first night when Rixon had abandoned that red-haired girl for her.

'Don't dance in here, this room's too small.'

'In the kitchen then?'

'No, not in there, you'll break something. This is a very small house. It's the smallest house I've ever lived in. It was built hundreds and hundreds of years ago. People were smaller then.'

'Where can I dance then?'

He pouted, sticking out his lower lip as if he were a child. Della tried to imagine all the people who had lived in the house, the monks who built the centre of it as a shelter from the storms, the farmers who had added extra rooms on here and there. The poor Thompsons who had sacrificed their limbs and necks for it and who now were said to haunt it. What pagan rites had been practised between these thick walls?

'Where—can—I—dance—then?' The boy approached her: a giant. There was too much of him. He was too big for a house like this.

Della tried to think of an answer, a sensible reply. People danced in ballrooms and in restaurants where there was floor space, they danced in dance halls, discothèques, but it was no good telling the boy that. He would not fit into any of these places any more than he fitted into this house. Girls would shy away from him; there was no point in suggesting a place where there were girls. 'You can dance in the fields when the snow

[41]

goes.' The music from the transistor drummed in her ears. 'Yes, you can dance in the fields to your heart's content.'

The boy's angry eyes stared at her, not quite straight on. He stayed stock still for a moment and then he switched off his transistor. He went into the kitchen and sat at the kitchen table, clanging his spoon against the cup of coffee she had poured for him, cold now. He clanged and clanged until he jerked the cup so that the coffee spilled over onto the table. Della took a cloth in her hand. 'It's no use losing your temper. This house just isn't big enough,' she said, by way of explanation. 'Not big enough for a boy like you. You're tall. You're as tall as Mr Rixon, maybe taller, and you don't see him jitterbugging around in here do you? Do you?' She wound the cloth round her fingers. 'You've got such long arms and legs. This place isn't big enough, not if you're going to dance and sing.' She went towards the spilt coffee, but the boy's elbow pushed her away. 'I did plan to have a bigger room built on. I said: "I'll never live in such a poky house." But somehow the money for the alterations got all swallowed up. I'd thought of a sunroom, something nice, where Hugh could sit and read his books and where he could talk to his friends if ever any of them came here to stay. A nice roomy place to make it all more reasonable. As it is, there isn't enough room to swing a cat: there really isn't any room at all.' The spilled coffee was spreading out, but even though she still had the cloth wrapped around her fingers ready to wipe it, it seemed unwise to approach it again. 'This place is claustrophobic, Daniel. I don't suppose you know what that means. It means the place gets on top of you, makes you feel shut in. Have you ever been in a lift when it breaks down, that's what I mean.' And immediately the thought came back to her of the ride in the high speed lift up to Robinette's office suite, the day the telegram came to tell her that Eugene was dead. 'Closed in.' Like in a grave. 'I suppose that's why Hugh's always so glad to get away. There's no room for grown-up boys like Hugh.'

The boy stretched out his long legs under the table. He planted his big feet on the floor, they did not move at all. There

[42]

was no sound. The house was silent, even the ticking of the clock was muffled. No sound at all, except for the boy's bony fingers, stabbing three angry crosses in the cold coffee he had spilled.

She went out of the house to escape the boy's evil mood. More snow was falling! The cat followed her to the doorstep. She saw it put out a paw to test the snow and then withdraw it hastily. The sheep were covered with snow. She shooed at them, wondering why they didn't move, why stay still and freeze? The horses sought what shelter they could against the buildings and the trees. There was noise coming from the cowhouses, maybe it was the bull. She did not investigate. She breathed in the cold snow-filled air, thanking God she had escaped from the house. She had given up smoking a long time ago. Old Robinette had disapproved of smoking, so she and Eugene had had to smoke secretly, puffing out through their bedroom window. She had given it up altogether after Eugene died, but sometimes now the desire for the taste of smoke came back. Why am I always thinking about Eugene? she asked herself. I must be getting old, always remembering the past. Though when was the time I didn't think about Eugene? She shivered and looked towards the road and wondered how Rixon would get the car up to the end of the drive when he came home. It might be necessary for the boy to go out and meet him, he could take a spade, dig a way for the car, vent his bad temper on the snow. Or maybe Rixon would have to abandon the car, walk to the farm. There's one thing, she reassured herself, nothing will keep him away. Nothing. No, not from me, she explained to some imaginary hearer. I'm not much of a draw, not any more. This place is what I'm talking about, this farm. Whatever the weather, this place will draw him home.

'I'll always come back to you,' he had once said. She smiled a little, thinking that it was only young men who made statements like that, young men who weren't really thinking what they said.

Then, thinking of those words on Rixon's lips, she began to

[43]

wonder if he had ever said it at all. Maybe it had been Eugene. Oh, to hell with Eugene, she thought. Not much of the day had gone by and there were hours to be got through before Rixon came home. Something came back to her of their first meetings, the meetings after he had deserted the red-haired girl for her. She smiled again and this time she was not thinking of Eugene.

There was steak in the freezer, fillet, saved for a special occasion, like if Hugh ever brought any of his Cambridge friends home unexpectedly. The son of the Labour peer, maybe? Well, she would defrost it, cook it for Rixon tonight. She looked around her, at the farm which Rixon had always wanted so badly. Now he's got it and I'll have to start making the best of it. She looked at the cold animals. I'll try to appreciate the farm like he does. I'll try to love the animals. Maybe I can grow to tolerate the bull. Tonight she would make a new start, she would cook green peas and asparagus and she would make one of those special sauces. She would open a bottle of wine and she would say: 'Sorry, Tom. I'm always a bit edgy when Hugh goes. But there's a lot to be said for being on our own.' Then she would say: 'I cabled old Robinette today and told him I couldn't think of flying out to the Caribbean. The poor old thing: he gets the craziest ideas. I'll write to him, tell him my place is here. As if I'd think of leaving *you*.'

The snow still fell, she licked it from her lips. There were many things to do before she cooked that meal she had planned. But even so, she could spare a moment to think about her plans: there were frozen mushrooms she had picked once on a morning walk. She wondered how well they had survived. She might use them for a garnish or a sauce. Her spirits lifted; this would be the first feast they had had for a very long time. She would think positively from now on, try to enjoy life more. Every day, I'll tell myself, in every way, life is getting better. But now she ought to go around the farm and inspect all the animals, do what she could for them.

It was getting harder to walk in the deepening snow, but Della stepped lightly. The snow brought back memories of the time before she married Rixon when she had gone all the way to Scotland to meet him. She remembered that she had hardly recognized him in his large greatcoat and his snow-covered forage cap. She remembered that she had been shy at the sight of him and that he had seemed worried about the impression that he might make on her. 'My God, Della,' he had said. 'I feel capable of anything now you've come back. We'll go a long way together you and me—' She had wiped the snow off Rixon's face with a tissue on that day when he had stood waiting for her. 'And I won't let any bloody American pinch you from me; not this time.'

A little of the old feeling, the feeling which had made her end her widowhood, stirred up in her now.

She would make an occasion of tonight. Of course, there was the boy. He would get in the way of the festivities. He would just have to go out somewhere; she would pay him to go down to the village, he could buy fish and chips for himself and eat them in the café. There must be some boys he could find to talk to. She would bribe him into letting her and her husband have a little time alone together. 'Tom,' she said, 'it's surprising the things that can happen to you on a day like this.'

The boy was in the living room when she got back. He was pouring Rixon's hair oil onto his head. A droplet of it ran down his forehead and down his twisted nose. She looked at his ugly face and his ugly sleeked-down hair and at his odd unprepossessing eyes. She found herself thinking of Hugh. The little pain struck her and then she thought of Rixon and of Eugene. She thought how all of them had been good looking in their different ways. The boy poured more of the oil onto his head.

'Daniel, Mr Rixon won't be pleased.'

'Why?'

'When he sees you with that hair oil on.'

His hands touched his sodden hair and his fingertips smoothed the parting he had made. 'He won't be seeing it, will he?'

'Not if you hide in the loft.' But again his ugliness was almost blotted out by the memory of the other faces. 'And even if he can't see it, he'll smell it. You can smell it all over the house. You'd better get it off.'

He grinned his irritating grin: 'Old Rixon won't be coming home.'

'Don't be silly.'

The boy swayed a little as if he might start the dance again, the dance which she had ended. The scent of Rixon's hair oil hit her hard as if her husband were already there, home from the bank, already in the room. The boy turned his back on her. He looked at himself in the mirror, pulling his crooked eyes into a smile, making his face more grotesque than she had ever seen it.

'Thought he'd got a medal from the King. Him with a medal and he can't even drive his rotten old car up here in the snow.'

She clutched at his sleeve: 'You mean he's telephoned?'

The boy pulled away: 'Said he daren't take the risk.'

She looked around her: 'You mean he's not coming home?'

'Kipping at his mother's.'

'But this is *his* farm. It isn't *my* farm. It's *his*.'

He combed his short oiled hair very carefully, patting it with one hand.

'And give me that comb. I've told you not to comb your hair in here.' The boy swung around and tightened his grip on the comb.

'I'll do as I like. I'm the boss. Old Rixon said so.'

The tug of war went on.

'Old Rixon said I'm Number One.'

'Did he?'

'Called me his manager.'

'You don't say.'

'Put me in charge.'

'Well, well.'

It would take a bottle of shampoo to get that oil out of his hair. Rixon's oil, a present she had bought for him.

'I told him about you bringing them woolly bastards down.

Told him you wouldn't take no notice of me. He said: "I'll have something to say about that when I get home." '

The teeth of the comb dug into her hands. 'And I'll have something to say to him.' She would tell him that she was tired of him discussing her with the boy. She would say that it was bad enough trying to handle him without Rixon paying him silly compliments, filling his head with nonsense. She would tell him that there was no place here for the boy. He goes or I go, she would say. It came to her that there would be no cosy supper that night, no steak, no asparagus, no wine. The feel of the oil and of the boy's hair on the comb sickened her. She let it go.

'When is he ringing back?'

The boy turned to the mirror and admired his greasy slicked-down hair. 'I told him I'd take care of things. I said I'd be a manager like he said. And he said: "Dan, I'm glad there's somebody with a bit of sense at that farm. Somebody who can keep an eye on things." '

❦❦

Rixon with his army-cropped hair looked down from the mantelpiece. His handsome face grinned at her. 'Just so long as we can be together,' his fine eyes said.

She sorted through her old bank books, cheque stubs, statements. 'It hurts me to let you put in so much of your money, Dell.' Twenty-five thousand towards the purchase price of the farm, seven thousand five hundred towards the stock and three hundred and twenty-five guineas towards the bull. Eugene's inheritance all gone: the sale price of his maternal grandfather's tidy little mill all ploughed into a barren English plot. 'Down the Swanee, Eugene, as they say. Almost every red cent turned over to Tom or to Hugh. And do I hear you ask what there is in it for me? Rows of gaping mouths to fill, frustration, privation and this snow.'

She had not yet been to see the bull. She had so far obeyed her

[47]

rule of leaving it for Rixon or the boy, but today Rixon was not coming home and she could not bring herself to ask the boy to do it. Let him stay in, flattening his odious hair.

The door to the bull's pen was badly hinged. Like every gate and door and fence on the farm it was neglected. She wondered how the farm would survive in a real storm. She looked at the bull, dividing it into pieces, bisecting it and cutting it across again. 'Three-quarters of you belongs to me, you monster. The worst investment I ever made.' She visualized a neat hairline down its back and down one flank, marking out her territory. 'And when I leave Tom, I'll ask for all of Eugene's money back and I'll insist I get my three-quarter share in you.'

Would Rixon be honourable? Would he give her her share of this ugly, malevolent beast? Did she want three-quarters of it? The bull was male and that was all it was. It was not gentle like the cows, it did not look straight at you. There was nothing human about it, nothing to make you identify with it, pity it, feel for it as you might the cows.

'You were the death of all my hopes. I knew as soon as Tom brought you here that he had flipped his lid. If you were any use at all, I'd accept it, all of it. He says: "What are you worrying about? We'll make a fortune in stud fees." How can a man with his acumen know so little about making money? How many cows will visit in this weather? And I don't think you'll be going far looking for business either. There'll be very few assignments for you in this snow.'

A shrill whistle sounded from behind her: the boy.

'Haven't you any more sense?'

He poked a stick towards the bull.

'Stop that, you fool.'

She filled up the hay trough and the water trough. The boy offered no help; he stood behind her, barring her way. He switched the stick in his hands. She looked at the bull fearfully.

'Stop it.'

He did not stop.

'I shan't tell you again.'

[48]

'My Uncle Charlie says you're crackers.'

'What a diagnostician. But I don't altogether disagree with him.'

'Says you're funny in your head, talking to cows and horses like you do.' He switched his stick again. 'Says you've no option, because no one else cares what you say.'

She approached the boy slowly, and for a moment she was afraid that he would not move aside to let her pass. A sense of anxiety invaded her; the boy in front and the bull behind her. 'I'm glad you're so impressed by Uncle Charlie. Because it solves a problem for me. We'll go inside and get your things together and then you can walk down to the village. The roads are good enough for that. There's a bus at three o'clock: you'll be on it. You can change onto the bus to Manchester and you'll be at your Uncle Charlie's in time for supper and you can listen to his witty sayings every day.' The boy stepped aside so suddenly that he stumbled and had to steady himself on the door. She looked back at the bull to see if it reacted to the noise, but it was eating turnips which had been sliced for it the night before. 'And let me remind you once and for all that most of this farm belongs to me and for that reason what I say goes.'

The boy did not stand straight up, he looked smaller than she had ever seen him look and he did not seem to have anything else to say about his Uncle Charlie. He started out through the door and then he stood back, holding it, so that Della could go out first. He stayed close to her on the way back and before they got there he said, as if it were very important that the words were said before they got into the house: 'Don't make me go back to my Uncle Charlie, Missus.'

She was silent and her body ached.

'I'll do all the work, I'll take care of all the cows and horses. I'll feed the bull. I'll do everything you say.'

She broke the silence: 'You can start by washing that foul oil out of your hair.'

'As soon as we get in, I will.'

'And if there's any more of your impudence—'

'I'll never answer back again.'

The drifting she had feared had begun. In the strong wind she was blown towards the boy. 'And another thing, next time the phone rings, just you come and get me. I don't care where I am.'

'I'll shout and shout until you come.'

It was not easy to communicate in this storm. She shouted her warnings and the boy shouted his promises back.

'Can I stay here then?'

There were two incontrovertible signs of madness in Rixon: the bull, the boy. She allowed her reply to be lost in the cross-current of the wind.

He worked well for what was left of the afternoon, chopping wood, vacuuming carpets, refilling containers with water, bringing coal into the house. He filled a saucer with milk for the cat and left the cat in peace to drink it.

'I told you, Missus. I'll do all the work,' he said from time to time.

Della spent the afternoon preparing for the snow siege which she felt might be coming. She thought of the postman's words and of the Thompsons: ghosts, as he had called them. Ghosts? She wished that there were such things, she wished that the ill-fated Thompson or his wife might alert her to the mistakes they had made thirty years ago, what erorrs had contributed to their tragic end. She felt that it was necessary for the food for the animals to be brought nearer to the house, that their water supply must be ensured. She checked the food in the freezer. That at least would hold out for a week. She pushed the precious fillet steak to one side.

The boy made coffee for her: he had, she saw, washed his hair, but she decided not to comment upon it.

At four o'clock she decided to telephone Rixon at the bank. There was no reply. Did that mean that he had already gone for the day? Had *his* work ended? She thought of him drinking tea from his mother's china cups and became a little angry.

Then the boy put on his best suit and his high-heeled cowboy boots and said that he was going out.

'Don't be silly.'

'I've done all the work, haven't I?'

'I don't care what you've done. You're not going anywhere in weather like this.'

He had tied Hugh's scarf around his neck; one side of it reached down to his knees.

'Daniel, sometimes I wonder if you *are* all there. You must be out of your mind. Take off Hugh's scarf and those silly shoes, because I have no intention of letting you go out in a blizzard. Not that I care what you do, but your Uncle Charlie would have something to say if you died of exposure on the roads.'

'I'm bloody well sixteen.'

'Yes, and I'm bloody well responsible for you.'

'I'll do as I like, I'm going out.'

His high heels would leave little holes in the ice. He would have to walk bent half double to shield himself from the wind. If he got as far as the village, there would be no hope of him coming back to the farm that night. She would be all alone with the Thompsons and their woes. Perhaps it might be better to be on her own: at least there would be no one to annoy her.

'That magistrate said I had to get some young friends. It makes me sick to be with old people all the time.'

'That magistrate put you in my care.' But she did not feel like another argument just now. Let him go, then at least she'd get some peace.

He flung the long end of Hugh's scarf around his neck again and stepped out, banging the door behind him, then he re-opened the door and looked back in. 'And I won't be back either. I'm off to Liverpool, and I'm going to get on a boat when I get there. So you won't be seeing me again.'

She got up and began to wash the dishes. The stillness of the house was disturbed by the violence of the winds. She had no

[51]

energy to go after him. And he *was* sixteen, as he had said. She supposed she ought to ring the social worker. After all, there was a supervision order on him. But she could not bring herself to do it. It would be awkward answering questions, explaining why his dead body was to be found a quarter of a mile from the house, hard to explain why he had gone out in high-heeled shoes, hard to explain why he was wearing a St John's scarf when he could hardly read and write a word. 'Those shoes—' she would tell the coroner, 'he saved up for weeks to buy them. He was inordinately proud of them. I never could persuade him to take them off.'

She dried the dishes very carefully. She knew that she should make an attempt to contact the police, the social worker, somebody, but lethargy filled her. She tried to imagine his dead body frozen in the snow, but it was hard to think of the boy dead. He was not the kind of boy who would die young. In any case in only a few minutes he was back. He came in, leaving the door open behind him.

'That was a very short evening out.'

'Don't see why I should bloody freeze for you.'

She was drying a blue cup, she made sure no hint of moisture remained on it. 'For me?'

'Well, you'd like to get rid of me, wouldn't you?'

She put down the cup. 'That's what I like about you, Daniel. Your perceptiveness. I told Mr Rixon: "I don't care about his laziness, his impudence, his foul temper, that intuitiveness makes up for it all." You have your finger on the pulse. The "bloody pulse" as you would call it.'

His face was angry.

'Close that door and take off those wet shoes.'

He pulled one of the shoes off and held it up momentarily like a weapon, maybe he would split her skull with it and then he could face the coroner instead of her: 'She had no respect for my boots' or 'The Missus fell whilst I was cleaning my cowboy boots, sir, and she caught her skull on the heel.'

'Now look here,' she said, poking at his chest with a wet

[52]

finger. 'Before we go any further with this mad Siberian charade, I'll give you one last warning. And don't,' she slammed the door shut, 'waste your breath on any arguments about the means of transport you'll use. You can crawl on your knees, slide on your backside, pedal your bicycle for all I care.'

He took off his other shoe and flung it on the floor. The cat fled under the chair, its usual hiding place.

The boy looked at Della with his crooked eyes and then he went upstairs.

The cat looked out at her and blinked its eyes. She rubbed its head until it purred: 'Don't worry about Captain Oates,' she said. 'If I know him, he'll stay out of our way for a very long time.'

At seven thirty Rixon phoned: 'The roads are terrible, Dell. You've never seen snow like there is down here.'

'Poor lamb, poor lamb.'

'So I daren't take the risk of trying to get the Mini up there. If I couldn't get back to the bank in the morning, I'd be for the high jump.'

'You'll have earned every tick of that rolled gold watch.'

'You all right, Dell? I've been worrying about you up there.'

'I've been worrying about *you*. I keep thinking of you, digging your way out of the bank.'

There was a brief silence and then Rixon said: 'You're still in that funny mood.'

'Funny? Me? What an adjective to use about me.'

Another silence.

'You still there, Dell?'

'Sadly, yes.'

'Is anything the matter?'

'What could be the matter with me?'

'Well, the boy? Is he behaving himself?'

'Perfectly. We're like a house on fire, you know that.'

The boy was still upstairs, there was no noise coming from his room. He must be sulking. He had left his transistor downstairs for once and he had not come down to get it. She had begun to worry about him now, she worried more than when he was out in the snow.

'What *is* the matter then?'

'What do you mean?'

'You sound odd, that's all.'

'I am odd. Let's face it. Odd as anything. I must have been odd to let you talk me into coming here. I must be more than odd to be stuck here on my own at this place, surrounded by mad bulls and mad boys. Would anyone who wasn't odd agree to stay here cut off from civilization?'

'It's not often we get snow like this. I'll be back tomorrow.'

To have given up my position as Robinette's daughter to marry Tom. Why didn't I stick to my guns? After all, if marrying Tom was such a good idea, why did I chicken out in the first place and run off with Eugene practically on the eve of the wedding?

'I expect you're a bit overwrought,' Rixon said. 'This weather's enough to upset anyone. There are cars off the road all over the place. I saw some pretty bad accidents on my way home.'

'Home?'

'Mother's.' He whispered the word. 'But you know I won't stay away from the farm any longer than I have to.'

'I know that all right.'

There was some sound from the boy's room. She was no longer listening to Rixon, she was thinking about the boy: I will, she decided, try different tactics in future. I'll try to be more understanding. I'll reason with him, instead of giving orders. I'll explain why I want him to do things, solicit his co-operation. After all, he is only a child and I don't suppose it's any more fun for him than it is for me.

'Well,' Rixon said. 'I'll ring again in the morning, make sure you're all right. Let's hope the weather clears by then.'

I'll appeal to his better nature in future, she said to herself, meaning the boy's better nature.

'Don't slip on the bank steps and break your neck,' she said, by way of goodbye.

Well, there were nice clean sheets on her bed, that was something. Not cotton either, she had put on flannelette for warmth. She kept the light on so that she could read her book and she thought that there were compensations in having no tired Rixon to ask her to turn it off. He liked the dark so that he could think about his farm with no distractions. For once, she had the bed all to herself. A large king-size bed. Second hand. Bought from the old vicar for ten pounds when he left the vicarage. No restless Rixon to share it, nothing to disturb her peace. Sleeping alone was an almost forgotten luxury. She could hear the boy's transistor now, he must have gone downstairs to get it. He played it as loudly as it would go. Well, that was all right, there were no neighbours to annoy and the bull wouldn't complain about a little music.

She read a page of her novel: the heroine had fallen out of love with her husband and she had fallen in love with a garage hand with calloused palms. The woman in a big, pale blue car paid for by her husband raced along the motorway to be embraced by those calloused hands. Della's flesh reacted a little at the thought of this. The garage hand, in a little yellow van borrowed from the garage where he worked, broke the speed limit.

Bloody fool, Della thought. She was thinking of the woman. Can't she find something better to do with her time and with her petrol, the price it is? There isn't a man alive who's worth a gallon of it. She remembered that she had not yet replied to Robinette's cable. Men always find some way of making you pay; they break your heart or your spirit or they spend all your money or they wear you out with work. Or they drive you mad with guilt, blaming you because you won't devote your life to replacing their lost sons. They can't understand that there are things you want yourself, quite normal things. And what were these normal things for which she had left Robinette and the house in Mimosa Street? The opportunity to follow Rixon around from army camp to army camp, from bank to bank and finally to end up in this cold hell hole. 'I want what all women want. You'll just have to understand,' she had told Robinette. A lunatic husband and a son who doesn't give a damn?

She laid down her book and put her hand out to Rixon's space, thinking of him. She tried to remember how she had once found his body exciting, she had once followed him for the same reason as the woman in the book followed the garage mechanic. Now all she thought was: All that space for me. She closed the book.

The music from the transistor seemed louder. She sighed and got out of bed and went to the boy's door. The supper she had left for him was still untouched outside his door, uneaten to pay her back.

She opened the door very quietly. He was, she saw, asleep, lying uncovered on his bed, the transistor held in his hand. She took it away from him and turned it off. His eyes were shut tight, his mouth wide open, a lock of his yellow hair covered his forehead. When he was asleep it was hard to see what there was about him that repelled her. She thought of waking him up, of telling him that he must undress properly, put on his pyjamas and get between the sheets. The wind was howling now, but she tried to put it from her mind. She covered the boy up with extra blankets. 'No point waking you up,' she insisted to him. 'Sleep all you can.' The house shook in the wind. 'So much for Tom's two-foot-thick walls! Get your sleep. Heaven only knows what lies ahead for you and me.'

Back in her own room, she found that she could not sleep at all, in spite of the luxury of the empty bed. The wind had always frightened her. If Eugene had lived, she would not be alone now, or at any rate she would not be alone in a ten pound, second-hand bed. As other people counted sheep, she now began to count beds, the many beds she had slept in with Eugene. They had shared a multitude of beds in their short married life. There was the bed at the St Regis on their honeymoon, the series of motel beds on the journey south and the four-poster in Mimosa Street, to name a few. It became important to her to remember every one of them. What was the name of that wild piece of coast off North Carolina? The place where they had dropped anchor on the old man's boat? I'm beginning to forget, she thought. It's all being driven out of my mind by this place. 'Eugene,' she whispered, 'it seems to me that I've never been really happy since the day you died. It seems to me that I've got less and less happy every day.' She became afraid that she had spoken so loudly that the boy could have heard her. Nonsense, he's sound asleep, she told herself. And, in any case, the fierce wind drowned out every sound within the house. 'Eugene, don't go away.' With Rixon out of the way, she could allow the tears to spill from her eyes, 'So long as I can feel you're with me, I can carry on, however terrible life gets at this place.' At last, in spite of her thoughts and of the terrifying wind, sleep did begin to overtake her.

There had, she remembered, been one bed before the St Regis. She thought of it sadly. Only one.

'Goodnight, Eugene,' her silent, sad voice said.

'Oh my God!' Della screamed. She went downstairs in her dressing gown to make an early morning cup of tea. The solid blackness at the window had risen; there was no looking out now.

'Daniel!' she shouted. 'Get up. Come down here. Look at the snow. It's solid against the windows.' Fear of being imprisoned drove her to unlock the door and open it, to find some means of escape. She turned the key and pulled the door open and a bank of snow invaded the room. She tried to push the door back, her body struggled against it. 'Daniel!' she screamed again. 'For God's sake, come down.'

The still sound of the snow rang in her ears. 'Daniel, damn you. Hurry up.' She shouted as loudly as she could to break the silence. She listened and at last she heard his footsteps overhead.

[57]

'Please, Daniel. Please.' The bank of snow was coming in on her, crushing her back. 'Daniel, Daniel. Oh, dear God.'

His feet came down the staircase slowly; no part of him was capable of activity at this time of day. The curtain at the foot of the stairs moved this way and that and finally his head came through it. 'For God's sake, Daniel. Help me.' He rubbed a knuckle at his eyes. He had slept in his clothes she remembered and now his shirt was unbuttoned and it was not tucked into his trousers. She had told him over and over again not to come downstairs half dressed. Even now his dishevelled state annoyed her.

'Help me with this door.'

'What's the matter with it?'

'Why don't you use your eyes?' He rubbed his eyes again, violently, not really seeing her. He stood in the middle of the room, disconnected like a sleep walker.

'Help me.'

'What?'

The door moved in against her, driving her into the room, closer to the boy. His head moved now from side to side as if he could not quite understand.

'There's been more snow in the night. If we don't get this door shut, we shall freeze to death. Do you understand?'

He woke up and came and stood quite close to her, watching her. His big hands clasped and unclasped helplessly.

'You'll never get it shut, Missus. There's too much snow, it's fallen in.' He was frightened and the sense of fear made *her* more frightened still. She became afraid to move in case the bank of snow moved in on her.

'Push,' her voice pleaded with him.

And now he unclasped his hands and he stood over her, pushing with all his force against the door. He was so close to her that she felt that she might be trapped, sandwiched in on one side by the snow and on the other side by the boy. It was the same feeling that she had experienced in the bull's pen.

'It isn't any use,' she said, whispering because the boy's

[58]

nearness made normal speech inappropriate and because the snow opposed them like some living, moving thing against whom it was necessary that they should conspire. 'It's no good,' she told the boy. 'Because if we go on pushing all that will happen is that the door will crack and break in two. We'll never get it shut.'

She smelt the smell of the boy's body too close to hers and she decided that she might suffocate because of the young male smell, but then he moved away from her and stood looking at his hands, as if he were afraid of them because they had been no use against the snow.

After the boy had moved away, she stayed spread-eagled against the door for a minute and then she gained courage and walked away from it slowly. Some of the snow fell into the room. She looked back quickly, the door was wedged open for maybe a foot. She felt as if her back and limbs might break and as if her spirit had broken already.

'Why did I open the door?' she said aloud.

'I don't know, Missus. Why did you?'

'Don't ask questions.'

'It's all right, Missus,' the boy said, stammering again. 'I'll get the shovel and I'll dig it all away.'

'Don't be silly.' But perhaps he *could* dig it away.

'I'll dig it all away and,' his eyes turned towards the kitchen, 'I'll melt it all in the sink.'

'Daniel, there must be tons of snow. If you dig away the surface, more will come in.' But if they left it alone, undisturbed, what would happen then? The boy took a handful of snow and moulded it into a snowball, he took aim as if to throw it but then changed his mind and let it fall.

'Will we be all right, Missus?'

'What do you mean?'

'Will we freeze to death like you said?'

'Nothing to worry about at all.' She watched the melting snow left over from the snowball dripping from his hand.

'We'll be able to breathe, won't we?'

[59]

'I've been in worse snows than this.' But would the snow swallow all their air? 'Eskimos live in snow houses, don't they?'

'I'm scared,' the boy said.

'Scared? What nonsense.' She looked at his white face. 'I'm not scared. It takes more than a few feet of snow to worry me.' She breathed on her cold hands. 'I know what I'll do, I'll pack the gap up with blankets. I'll nail them to the wall, then we'll be all right.'

The boy wandered to the window: 'How will we get out? You can't see anything out of here.'

'Don't open any windows.'

He wheeled around: '*I* didn't open the *door*, did I? *You* did. You blame me for everything.' He rubbed at the glass. 'I'm not silly.' He went on rubbing at the window as if by rubbing on the inside he might get rid of the dense snow outside. His breath left a layer of steam and he drew one of his crosses in it, slowly and carefully as if he were inscribing a message of great moment. Then he said: 'We won't be able to get out of the door, Missus?'

'Not unless we burrow out like rabbits.'

'We might get out all right if we had a back door.'

'Possibly, but as we haven't one, we'll have to think again.'

'Why haven't we got a back door?'

'Why haven't we got anything sensible?'

She sighed. She had begged Rixon to have a back door made and, more than that, she had reasoned that there should be access from the house to the cowhouses so that there would always be an easy way to feed the cattle. The boy was looking sideways at her again. She said: 'I'm not sure a back door would be much help, there's probably as much snow at the back. And there's nothing to stop the drifts at the back, no trees, nothing. Just those deserted moors.' They both tried to look out of the kitchen window. 'You see, I'm right. It's probably half-way up the back of the house.' But it remained true that a door to the cowhouse would be of great value, something else she had been denied.

'Will they come and dig us out?'

'I daresay. Or the snow will melt as soon as the sun comes up.'
'How will we know?'
'Know what?'
'About the sun?'
'Please, Daniel. I want to think. I've enough on my mind without you thinking up problems.' And then she said: '*We'll* be all right. We've got food and water. What I'm worried about is the animals. One of us will have to get out to them.' The boy looked at the door. 'No, there's no point in looking there. I know what, you go upstairs and see if there's a window you'd be able to get out of.' The boy looked at her silently, he spoke less when he was frightened. 'Go upstairs: go on.' She put a hand out as if to push him, but the hand did not quite reach him. 'The old parson's bed came in through a bedroom window, it would never have gone up the stairs, so if a wide bed like that could go in, you must be able to go out. You're big and bony but you're thin.' The boy looked at his big body, his thumbs and first fingers pressed together as if he were measuring something. At last he turned, or half-turned, becoming entangled in the curtain because he could not bear to let her out of his sight, but then his bare feet disappeared up the stairs. 'And put your shoes and socks on before you come back, it's bitterly cold down here.'

Bare feet. Old Robinette could not bear to see bare feet, he trembled lest nails, ants, mites or worse should get at his son's feet: BEG YOU ON NO ACCOUNT ABANDON FOOTWEAR IN HOTELS STOP EVEN HIGH CLASS HOTELS NOT FREE FROM INFESTATIONS LEFT BY FOREIGN FEET. The old man had a theory that small organisms travelled in the soles of the feet of potentates who travelled from Eastern climes and that these organisms might creep up your veins and damage your heart or brain. Such cables followed them to every motel and hotel they told him of on their honeymoon journey south. And something of it had stuck: WARN YOUR BRIDE NEVER TO GO BAREFOOT STOP DISASTERS MAY ENSUE. She called up to the boy: 'And remember what I said about your feet.'

The boy half-descended the stairs: 'What?'

[61]

'Your shoes, put on your shoes.'

'I've bloody got them on,' he shouted back, 'and you needn't think I'm going out of the landing window either, it's not big enough for a worm.'

She sighed: 'All I asked you to do is to find one you can get out of. I'm busy blocking up the door.'

Her hands were shaking and she shivered with something from inside her, not the battle with the door and not the coldness of the air, something else. It was too early to telephone Rixon but even so she picked up the telephone and dialled his number. It rang. She had feared that the snow might have destroyed the cables, but so far they were intact. She took blankets from a blanket box and put one of them around her shoulders for warmth. Then she plugged in the electric kettle and found that the electricity supply was still intact. The boy's heavy feet tramped through the upstairs rooms. Occasionally he shouted down: 'This 'uns blocked, Missus. That'ns black as night.' A giant barometer happily predicting gloom. His voice was cheerful, he laughed at each new sign that they were trapped in the house. The kettle boiled, she stared at the steam and wondered if she could still her shaking hands for long enough to deal with it. The boy's voice came down again: 'All of 'ems blocked up with snow.' The doubts she had always had about him magnified. Did he know what the blocked windows might mean? Did he realize that they might perish in this snow like the Thompsons? Did he care? Might he even welcome extinction? No more magistrates, no more social workers, no ugly face looking out at him from the looking glass, no more angry words from Della, no more loneliness in the billiard room. He came downstairs, his face was bright.

'Missus, they'll have to dig us out and helicopter us away.'

'Yes, I expect they'll do that,' she said and her mind sought comfort. After all, as she had said, Eskimos survived in igloos. They complained bitterly when they were put in houses. But did igloos have some kind of ventilation? Or did the air come in through the snow? What about sheep who got buried in the snow? They frisked out, large as life days later. She spooned tea into the pot, one spoon for her, one spoon for the boy and another one—for whom? Who was there who gave a damn? Would Rixon come and dig them out if they were trapped? What about Hugh with his brains and his bloody education? What about Eugene: where was he when she needed him? Why had he met that shell, head-on? Why hadn't he got out of the way, used his eyes, seen the danger? What about the police, the fire services, the R.A.F.?

She handed a cup of tea to the boy and saw that he was grinning.

'Don't laugh, Daniel. If you're not worried about us, what about those poor animals? I don't know what will happen to them.' If she had enough steam, she could melt the snow, rout it, sending it rushing down the hill. But there was nothing, just the boy and he knew nothing except joy-riding in stolen cars, destroying and annoying. He was back at the foot of the stairs, half covered by the curtain, grinning, fingers snapping to a silent tune.

'Leave that curtain alone, Daniel. You'll have it down.'

'I've been kidding.'

'What?'

'I've found one. I've found a window I can get out of. I've been out of it just now. Your bedroom—'

From habit she wanted to tell him that she had told him time and time again to keep out of her bedroom, but she stopped herself, saying only: 'I told you not to open any windows.'

'Couldn't see out unless.'

She poured another cup of tea with her still shaking hands. There were advantages in the boy's spiky frame. She began to measure out the porridge oats. Better make sure he was strong and warm before the time came for him to venture out. The telephone rang.

'ANTIDOTE TO PORCINE FLU MORE DANGEROUS THAN DISEASE ITSELF STOP SHUN.'

'Are *you* telling me that or is *he*?'

'Him, of course,' the Western Union Man said. 'I've never even heard of Porcine Flu.'

'Is there an epidemic?'

'That's not stated in the cable. But whatever it is, you've got your instructions. Shun it.'

'The disease or the antidote? I don't think he makes that clear. Does he say anything else?'

'Only: HOPE RIXON WELL. But I get the feeling he doesn't really wish Rixon well at all.'

'How can you tell that?'

'When you've handled as many cables as I have—'

'You can tell by the feel of them.'

'You get to know the tone of voice. Take Mr Robinette: elderly, educated, anxious, accent wavers between the Deep South and New England?'

'Do you have a high ratio of success with your predictions?'

'I never get the opportunity to check.'

'I can't talk for long. We're snowed up and the boy is about to step out of the upstairs window.'

'Suicide?'

'Self-preservation. The preparations for it are reminiscent of the ones taken by the first man on the moon. I'll have to go and hurry him up or the animals will starve to death. It's past their breakfast time. I'll talk to you later.'

The boy was looking forward to his climb out of the window and he was looking forward to his slide on the snowbank. 'I'll go on my stomach,' he said.

'You'll do no such thing.'

'I will.'

'You won't.' She tried to listen to the news on her transistor, but a song from his drowned out hers. Even so, fragments of the news came to her. 'Gale force winds', 'severe drifting', 'farms cut off—' 'So try to be sensible. If you go on your stomach you risk cracking your skull. And in addition, you won't be able to see where you're going.' She snatched at his sleeve to make him listen. He pulled away from her, smiling, the kind of smile he must have had when he'd stuck one of his nasty pieces of wire in the lock of a car. 'What's the use of talking?' she asked. She pulled him forward by the lapels of his jacket, insisting that he do up all the buttons. 'Now you've got all the instructions clear, haven't you? Go into the cowhouse and shout as soon as you get there, then I'll know that you're all right. Give them their feed and water, give them as much as you can. Then feed the bull, and for God's sake, don't play the fool with it. I'm surprised it hasn't gored you before now the way you play around.'

'That crazy bull.'

'Crazy or not, just give it its feed and water and then get out.' She tied Hugh's college scarf about his neck.

'You're choking me.'

'Good. And when you've fed the bull and watered it, come out and shout again. Do you hear me? Let the dogs out for a while, let them run around then feed them and put them back and give the sheep and horses plenty of hay and then shout all the way back. I'll have the old clothes line ready in case you want pulling up.'

'Do you want me to clean out the cowhouse?'

'You'd better, but leave the bull's shed alone. Just give it its food and water and then get out like I said. I don't trust you with the bull.'

He began to dance like a matador, using his old anorak like a cloak. Then he put the anorak down and began to undo and retie Hugh's scarf, not for warmth, but elaborately, for decoration. He tied it as carefully as if he were Hugh with one of his cravats. Then he combed his yellow hair.

'A little of my Worth perfume perhaps?'

He giggled, one of his hands upon his head.

'In case you meet a milkmaid in the cowhouse.'

'A milkmaid, Missus?' He turned over the idea.

When he had some project in his mind, his crooked eyes shone like a child's eyes. She made him put a woolly hat on his head.

'You're squeezing my brains out and you're flattening my

hair.' With none of his thatch of hair showing, he looked worse than usual. If he did bump into a milkmaid, it would avail him nothing. He pulled a few strands of his awful hair out of the cap. 'I wish I'd never let you bloody scalp me last week.'

'By the time you actually get outside the house, your hair will have grown into ringlets half-way down your back.' She pushed him, not gently, to the foot of the stairs. He began to shake with laughter. Up the stairs, into her bedroom, which she had said he must never enter, and to the window. 'Now, you've got it all straight, haven't you? You know exactly when to shout? The whole operation shouldn't take you more than three-quarters of an hour. No, if you're going to clean out the cows, maybe a full hour. No teasing the bull and no dilly-dallying with the milk-maids.'

He was still laughing and he saluted her and then she saw that he was wearing the cowboy boots.

'You're not going in those. You'll trip on something and break your neck. If you won't take them off, you're not going at all.'

He weighed the pros and cons. She pushed him down on the old vicar's bed and then she went to get his wellington boots and made him put them on.

'Can you be trusted to do as I say?'

He laughed his uncontrollable laugh and, at that moment, she caught sight of the two of them in the stained mirror of the dressing table, the boy's ridiculous laughing face and her own pale tired one. This is no time to worry about your looks, she reprimanded herself, but where in the world have they gone? Where was the pretty face, sought after by the vicar's son, by Rixon and by Eugene. Who *was* the woman in the bedroom wrestling with this ugly boy?

His flailing awkward limbs hit against the window frame and then at last he managed to sit down in the snow. His laughter had stopped and the coldness of the snow had shocked him.

'It's dark,' he said. 'I don't like it, it's not like daytime.'

She gave him the flashlight which she kept near to her bed and immediately he dropped it. She leaned out to retrieve it and wiped it dry: 'And remember everything I've said. Keep away from the back feet of the horses, they're always nervous when the weather changes especially in winds like this.' He switched the flashlight off and on, flashing the light up at the dense sky. 'And don't waste that, it's the only one I've got, the other is in Mr Rixon's car.' The light flashed again. 'Why do I have tell you everything twice?'

He stretched his legs out and looked at them as if he were going on a long journey and needed to decide if they would make it.

'And remember about the shouts.'

He drew another circle of light, illuminating the falling snow. Then he shouted three times: 'Yahoo, yahoo, yahoo.' He set off, sliding swiftly down the snowbank. 'I'm here, Missus, I've done it.' She thanked God that the snow had held him, that the layer of ice had not given way under his weight. A rebel voice inside her reminded her that it wouldn't matter if it had; he was, after all, a boy nobody wanted. A boy nobody might ever want. Even so, she withdrew her stiff frozen fingers from the window pane and crossed them, hoping his erratic progress would last. She hugged herself to keep warm, not daring to move until she heard another of his calls. The annoying name by which he always called her, 'Missus', would be welcome now. I'll never again complain about it, I'll never tell him to call me Mrs Rixon. When he comes back, I'll treat him with more respect. I'll spend the time whilst we're trapped in here teaching him to read and write. I know I keep making resolutions like that and that something always goes wrong, but this time I'll take him and myself in hand. I'll take up the lessons where Hugh left off. She could not see him now, he was probably in the cowshed, he had not shouted. She was slightly angry, alarmed, afraid. She drummed her fingers against her arm. She was not afraid for herself she realized, but afraid in the way she had been for Rixon on the battlefield, for Eugene in Korea and for Hugh when he set off in the old Fiat in that terrible icy weather. When was that?

Yesterday? And it was like the time Hugh took up rugger and later go-kart racing and like that terrible time when he had pneumonia. There has always, she complained to herself, been someone making me afraid. And now she and the boy were going to die like the Thompsons in this snow? You're exaggerating, as usual, she chided herself. What chance is there of that?

She noticed that there was a slight imprint of the boy's body at the top of the snowbank, a black cut-out form, ridiculous, like a character from his favourite cartoon: Tom? Jerry? A silly silhouette. She screwed up her eyes, trying to see what she could of Rixon's Folly, the bit of frozen earth to which he had dedicated his life. But why have I gone along with it? she wondered. What made me come back to England when he asked me to? Why didn't I stay put in Mimosa Street? Why didn't I stay on that train in Scotland all those years ago? I should have left him standing there on that platform. I left him standing once before; I must have been mad to come back to him as I did. And then she heard the next of the boy's cries: 'Missus, Missus!' He had forgotten the Yahoo, or she had missed it.

'Yes, I'm here. Are you all right?'

He shouted something else, but she could not catch what it was. His voice seemed weak and she could not hear it clearly. Had he tripped and fallen in the snow somewhere? Was he frozen, fatigued, frostbitten? But then there was another call.

'Mis*sus*.' The syllables of the word were attenuated, drawn out.

'What's the matter? Say where you are.'

'Here. I'm here.'

'Here? Where is *here*?'

If only he would walk instead of run, if only he would look where he was going, if only he would listen to the things she said. If only he would do as he was told, feed the animals, walk the dogs, leave the bull alone. If only he would use his head. Inside the house a bell rang. She started, not recognizing the sound, reacting to it fearfully as if it were a signal she had dreaded, some bad news from the boy. Then she identified it as

[68]

the telephone. Well, it would have to ring, there was no hope of her leaving the window until the boy came back. In any case, it must be Rixon, it had his usual, insistent nagging tone. 'You can do the waiting for once, Tom,' she shouted aloud at the telephone. 'I've done plenty of it myself all these years.' The ringing went on. 'Shut up,' she yelled and the telephone obeyed her. There was no noise at all now, nothing. She looked at her watch. Half an hour had gone already, half of the time she had allocated. So why am I worrying? But then she thought of his gangly body, maybe trampled by the bull or by the horses. Her voice wailed: 'Daniel!' He might have fallen on the ice, he might have broken an arm, a leg, a rib. 'Where are you?' Her thoughts insisted that terrible things don't happen, but then she argued: What about Eugene? What about those poor soldiers on that train? What about that Mr Thompson and his frozen wife? She took off her watch and listened to it to make sure it was ticking. She wound it, reassuring herself that it was ridiculous to worry until the full hour was up.

The telephone rang again. She put her hands over her ears until the ringing stopped.

The hands of her watch moved slowly. She shook her wrist to speed them up.

When more than the full hour had gone by, she took her own anorak out of the wardrobe and put it on the bed. The boy had not shouted as she had told him to; something must be wrong. She looked out of the window. It was light now, but she could see no sign of life. She told herself that she must be mad to have allowed a boy to climb out of an upstairs window in weather like this, particularly a boy without a brain in his head. She put on the anorak, but she did not wrap up warmly as she had insisted he should do. She advanced one foot out of the window, then she looked back at the vicar's bed, wondering if she should secure the clothes line to it. If the boy were injured, she might need some help in getting him back into the house. Would Rixon have the sense to send a search party to find them? It would have been wise to have answered Rixon's call, to let him know that the boy had not returned from outside. But she could not allow herself to waste time ringing him back. She began her climb, but as soon as she was fully outside the window she heard the boy's cry: 'Yahoo, Missus. I'm coming back.'

He appeared at the foot of the snowbank.

'You going somewhere, Missus?'

She stayed silent.

'It's cold down here.'

She sat back on the window-sill, barring his way. His clothes were sodden and he was shivering, she could hear that in his voice. He was still smiling his silly smile.

'Has it taken you all this time to feed the animals?'

'I've been cleaning out the cowshed as well.'

'It's nearly half past.' She pulled herself back in through the window and he scrambled after her.

'What the hell have you been doing?'

He lay down on the old vicar's bed.

His eyes were closed. He folded his arms across his chest as if he had frozen in the snow as she had feared. One of her violent desires to beat him to death rose up in her, exploding in her breast. She went toward him.

'Don't touch me, Missus. My body hurts with cold.'

'Touch you, you fiend. I'll murder you if you don't answer me.'

'Been feeding the cows like you said. Then I fed that crazy bull: it knocked the feed out of my hand. I didn't tease it neither. I fed the horses and the dogs and then I fed them woolly bastards, greedy as pigs they are.' He opened one of his eyes. 'Then I turned that old dustbin upside down and I covered it with snow. That old dustbin you said you didn't want. And I made a nice head for it and then I got some bits of coal.'

He was no longer wearing Hugh's scarf, she saw, that had gone. Why had it ever seemed likely that he might have died a dignified death? When he died, it would be from one of his idiotic tricks, he would parachute from the roof with an umbrella or make a snowman of himself; that was, if he escaped being murdered by one of the many people he set out to annoy.

'And then you put Hugh's scarf around its neck to keep it warm?' One of his hands crept up to his bare neck as if he were trying to recall what had happened to the scarf. 'And my flash-light, you left that outside in case the poor snowman couldn't see.'

'It *could* see. I made it two eyes out of coal.'

She narrowed her own eyes and she looked at his cheerful, silly face and at the hand which still felt at his neck and in spite of her loathing of him, she felt again the strong desire to dig her broken finger-nails into his neck. She clenched her hands. 'You demon,' she said. 'I don't suppose it ever occurred to you that I'd be in here going mad with worry whilst you were fooling about outside.' She grabbed hold of his arm, trying to drag him off the bed. 'And get off my bed with your rotten, soaking clothes.'

He pulled away from her and he looked at her seriously. He was not frightened but she had managed to chase the grin from his face: 'You better stop that, Missus. You came close to breaking my arm off.' He rubbed his shoulder. 'In any case, you stop bossing me about, this is old Rixon's bed as much as yours.'

Her fingers flexed, but then the telephone rang again. It must be telepathy on someone's part, she thought. Because if that telephone hadn't rung just now, I'm not altogether sure I could have stopped myself from strangling him.

Rixon telephoning from the bank, closed up in his warm office for privacy. She tried to remember whether the fuel regulations were still in force. Sixty degrees? Well, that wasn't bad, at least the *bank* doors were not wedged ajar by snow, with blankets the only protection from an avalanche. A cosy office in which he dispensed charm and advice.

[71]

'What the hell is going on?' he asked, forgetting about the charm for which he was known.

'Going on, Tom?'

'Where have you been?'

'Ah yes, I thought you might be wondering that.'

'I've rung three times or more.'

'Now, Tom, it's not good for a man of your age to get upset. Try to count to ten before you speak. They say there's less wear and tear on your arteries if you do. *I've* been employing that method of staying calm for years. You may have noticed it; that slight hissing sound under my breath.'

'Stop talking nonsense and tell me where you've been.'

The boy had followed her downstairs, he stood watching her as she talked, worrying that she might tell Rixon he must go.

'Oh, here and there. Daniel and I have been outside, we've been making a snowman. You know that old dustbin? I wanted to get rid of it, but you said we'd find a use for it; well, as usual, *you* were right. We put it upside down, of course. I know that using a base is cheating, you're supposed to use solid snow, but I always believe in cutting corners. And I've had plenty of practice in economy over the years. Then we tied Hugh's scarf around its neck; I like a snowman with a bit of class. That's why we used a St John's scarf, if we'd only cared about warmth I could have given it one of yours. I promised Daniel I'd ask if we could use that old pipe of yours. I never feel a snowman *is* a snowman without a pipe in his mouth.'

The boy stared at her, mouth falling open, crooked to one side. His clothes were soaking wet and she could not think how she would find enough dry clothes to keep him going in the storm.

'Are you still there?' Rixon asked.

'Yes, dear. Of course I am.'

'Well in future, will you please pick up the damned phone when I ring instead of fooling about.'

'Making a snowman with Daniel? You call that fooling about?

[72]

You said only the other day I should try to understand him, use a bit of child psychology, you said. You told me I was to remember that all work and no play—'

'You know damn well what I'm talking about.'

'In a way I do, but on the other hand—'

'I've had a pig of a morning.'

'Oh dear, I am sorry to hear that.'

'And a terrible night. I had to sleep on the bed settee. You know what I'm like, I can't rest in a strange bed, let alone a bed settee. Mother wanted to give me her bed, but I could hardly allow that.'

She began to tot up in her mind how many nights she had been privileged to sleep alone in the years since they had married. A few times whilst he was still in the army and posted away too far for her to join him, the whole month before Hugh was born because he complained that she was restless and that she disturbed his sleep, then odd nights since when he was away at conferences and once for two whole weeks when he had to have his appendix out. On the whole there had been years of bed sharing, listening to his nocturnal anxieties, his get-rich schemes, his farming dreams, late night discussions of farm indices, arguments for and against the rotation of crops, contingency plans for this and that.

'I can never sleep without you. And then I couldn't seem to stop worrying about you,' he said. When Rixon talked on the telephone he always stood up as if he were talking on a field telephone, as if the bank were a battlefield. She had never seen him put his feet up on his desk like business men in movies did. He spoke with urgency, he was always at the ready. Yes, sir, Rixon was alert, ready to spring. And whilst he talked his eyes moved rapidly from side to side. He was, he said, a wild animal trapped inside a bank. She changed the receiver to the other ear. 'So will you please tell me what's really been going on, then I can get on with my work with a quiet mind.'

'You'll see the snowman for yourself, unless there's a sudden rapid thaw. A work of art it is.'

'Della, please. I'm having a terrible morning here, don't make it worse with your puerile jokes.'

A terrible morning at the warm bank: clerks to reprimand, heads tossed, union action threatened, the bank rate up, the index down, guns pointing at the grids, skirts getting longer, credit shorter, things ain't what they used to be.

And yet in spite of the thoughts that came into her mind, thoughts like these, she did allow there was that tenderness she felt for him. If there was no tenderness, why should she have turned over all that money? 'Dear, dear—' she said.

'Are you being sarcastic, Della?'

'Sarcastic? Because I said "Dear, dear"?'

He had never wanted to work in a bank. He had told her that a thousand times. He had never wanted to go into the army either. He had never wanted anything but to be a farmer.

'You tend to sound sarcastic.'

The bank was more soul-destroying than the army, in the army you felt you were achieving something. Part of the time, at least.

'Sorry, I don't mean to. Well, I didn't mean to *then* anyway.'

One of the boy's blue hands stole out towards the fire. He moved it quietly and slowly as if he were afraid to draw attention to himself. His large wrist bones were awkward, youthful. She wished that she could end the telephone call so that she could do something about him, something to make him warm. There was a sudden change in Rixon's tone, someone must have come into the room and he did not want them to know that he was telephoning his wife in the bank's time.

'Just checking on the market,' she heard him say and then to her: 'Number Two's toeing the line, I trust.'

'Number Two? The boy?'

The coldness in the boy's bones was thawing out and colour was coming back into his face. His look was guarded. Did he fear that she might in fact murder him once the telephone call was over?'

'Well, if everything's all right.'

'A 1, Captain. Shipshape. Backs firmly to the wheel.'

She heard a click of the tongue from Rixon: 'Tut, tut, tut.'

'Bye-bye, Skipper,' Della said. And then there was another click of the receiver as Rixon slammed it down.

She gave the boy a pair of Rixon's pyjamas.

'Them's new.'

'Yes, they are. They were his Christmas present from Hugh.' She broke the seal on the polythene wrapping with a finger-nail. 'I'll sort out some dry clothes for you: you'll have to wear these until I've got them ready.'

'Old Rixon's brand new 'jamas.'

'Well, he's hardly likely to want to wear them at the bank and he won't need them at his mother's. She keeps a set of clothes for him at her house, she's always hoping there'll be a flood or a fire so he can't come home here.'

She poured him a measure of Rixon's brandy to warm his cold young blood and when he complained about the taste she let him drink it from Rixon's Baden-Baden mug. It played 'Deutschland uber alles' as he put it to his lips.

'Me drinking out of old Rixon's music mug.'

'*Mr* Rixon, please.'

She looked at Rixon's face on the mantelpiece. 'Have you ever heard of Clark Gable, Daniel? On television, do you remember? Well, a lot of people used to think Mr Rixon looked just like him. He was supposed to look just like a film star; some people said he was more like Gary Cooper.' She had seen a lot of those movie stars in Rixon's face and she could see them in the photograph even now. Black hair, those good eyes and that deep cleft in his chin. 'They used to say he could have been a film star if he'd been in Hollywood.'

The boy half closed his eyes: 'Old Rixon a film star?'

'Film stars were different in those days, they were chosen for their good looks. There was a certain type of handsomeness in fashion in those days.'

[75]

'Old Rixon could have been a film star?' He put a hand in front of his face to conceal a grin.

'What's so funny about that?'

'An old geezer like him.'

'He's not so old. He's fifty-eight. And in any case, I'm not talking about now. I'm talking about the time I met him when that photograph was taken.'

'He doesn't look like a film star to me.'

'Well,' Della said. 'I don't expect you to pay anybody any compliments. But I'm just telling you, that's what people used to say. Anyway, let's have those wet clothes off.'

The grin was wiped clean off his face: 'Not all of them—'

'Yes, all of them, you've got yourself soaked to the skin. And don't be so silly, you're not the first naked child I've ever seen. Here, you can put this towel round you, if you're so modest. Hurry up, you'll catch your death of cold.'

He looked at the towel, examined it closely, then tied it round his waist and let his sodden jeans fall to his feet. He pulled the pyjama trousers on. She turned her face away. Then she held the pyjama jacket out for him and turned to see his thin arms go into it. He was shivering, his teeth chattered so that it was difficult for him to speak.

'I'm frozen, Missus.'

'Yes, I know. You'll have to sit by the fire and I'll get you my Indian blanket to warm you up.'

'Was it from a real Indian?'

'I bought it from an Indian camp. It could have been made in Hong Kong for all I know, but the squaw who sold it to me said it was made on the reservation. Anyway, it's pure wool and it's warm, it's just the thing.'

His crooked face was serious.

'Missus?'

'Yes?'

'I won't make any more snowmen.'

'That's right. One is enough. Though I suppose somebody might as well get some fun out of the snow.'

[76]

'Next time I'll just climb outside and feed the cows and the bull and the dogs—' He might have been going to force himself to articulate the word 'sheep', but the telephone interrupted him. 'I'll work and work and work.'

The sleeves of Rixon's pyjamas were a little too long for him, they almost covered his hands. She signalled to him to fold them back. 'I'll never do anything silly from now on.'

'We'll see,' Della said, not hopefully.

'HOPE UNAFFECTED BY INCLEMENT WEATHER STOP,' the Western Union Man said. 'The blizzards must have hit the American news.'

'*This* weather won't make much news out there, they're used to blizzards and tornadoes. You'd think he'd have enough to do worrying about his own weather, wouldn't you?'

'I'm not so sure. Apart from the cables I haven't much experience of the States, except in pictures, of course. They're always getting snowed in in pictures.'

'Quite right. They have more than their share of wild weather.'

'Funny thing, I work for an American company but I've never set foot in the place.' The Western Union Man had some kind of Midlands accent. She had never noticed it before. She had always thought of him as Transatlantic, but now she listened very carefully to the vowels as he said his next few words: 'There is more. You're to beware of falling masonry and to avoid exposure in the snow. Then there's a stop. And after that he tells you to apply liniment to family chests. He obviously thinks that old remedies are the best.'

'Is that last word plural?'

'I haven't reached the last word yet. It goes on: STOP TENDEREST SOLICITATIONS ROBINETTE.'

A lump came into her throat: 'That plural baffles me.'

'I can check it out. We aim to please.'

'Don't bother. Are there any more?'

'A bumper crop today. But the next one puzzles me, I must admit.'

'Read it, I'm good at cracking codes.'

'Right then: REPLY RE CARIBBEAN AWAITED EAGERLY STOP CABLE ME PRONTO STOP.'

'No puzzle there, that's clear enough.'

'We haven't got to the mysterious bit yet. Can I ask a question?'

'Of course.'

'Is the old man a cowboy by trade?'

'Hardly.' She thought back to old Robinette and his London tailored suits; shantung for semi-tropical wear, fine gaberdine for town. 'Why do you want to know that?'

'It's the word "Pronto", he uses it a lot.'

'Maybe he's watched the same movies as you.'

'Could be the explanation. Hang on, there's more: SUFFERING GROUP STOP ATTRIBUTE TO ZERO WEATHER. Now that's the bit that really puzzles me: URGENT TO HAVE RESPITE FREEZING ZONES STOP. That word "Group"?'

'No problem there, the word is "grippe", *la grippe*. You don't know your *Guys and Dolls*. That's one picture you've missed. The old man peppered all his talk with French words. I remember someone else made that mistake once, we were in Alábama and the old man stopped a boy in the street and inquired if there was much *grippe* in those parts. I can tell you, the old fellow was so frightened of diseases, we'd have caught the next freight train out of there if he'd said "Yes". But instead he scratched his head and said: "No sir, we'm mostly individuals here." The old man borrowed a five dollar bill from me to tip that boy for saving him from the fear of flu.'

'Well, it sounds as if he's got it now.'

'It won't be flu, they say there isn't any about just now. But he must have got something, I suppose. Poor old Daddy.' And immediately she could visualize the old man, a thin old body wrapped in an Indian blanket like the boy's. Bolstered up by vitamin pills, antibiotics, hot water bottles, chest embalmed with liniment by his housekeeper. The old man had caught a dreaded feverish illness at last.

'There's still more. He must have money to burn: STRONGLY

[78]

DESIRE SEE YOU ONE MORE TIME STOP DESPERATE LONELINESS SINCE BOY WENT.'

She looked across at this boy, sitting, getting warm, with the Indian blanket around him. He still shivered a little. She tried to move closer to him, she pulled the telephone cord out as far as it would go so that she could reach him. But it was not long enough. 'Get nearer the fire, Daniel,' she whispered to him.

'HOPE YOUR BOY NEVER CAUSES YOU MISERY LIKE THIS.'

'Get nearer, Daniel,' she said.

'Sorry,' the man said.

'It's all right, I'm just talking to the boy. He's been out in the snow, making snowmen and he's come back soaked to the skin and now I'm trying to thaw him out. Better get him dry and warm or he'll be getting *la grippe* too.'

'He's a lucky boy.'

'In what way?'

'All alone at that farm with you.'

She looked at the snow-dark window: 'Not much fun to be snowed in.'

'I wouldn't mind.'

'I tell you it wouldn't be much fun.'

'I wouldn't say that,' the Western Union Man said and he sighed a long sigh. 'The cable ends by the way: NEVER REMOVE GALOSHES AND OTHER FOOT COVERINGS IN THE SNOW STOP NO PIECE OF THIS EARTH POLLUTION FREE. There is no "stop" this time, just his name: "Robinette". Shall I send these on?'

'Oh yes, but I doubt if there'll be deliveries here for days and days the way this weather looks. The postman is a very weather conscious man, he acts as a kind of weather vane in these parts. I don't think he'll venture here until there is no sign of ice. But please send them on anyway. And ring me immediately if there are any bulletins from Mr Robinette. I hope he's going to be all right.'

'You said yourself there isn't any real influenza about.'

'I know, but he's an old man. I don't like to think of him being unwell.'

[79]

'Well, I hope he's not too ill to send the cables. Gives me the chance to talk to you.'

'He'd have to be very ill before he'd desert Western Union. My first husband used to say it was the breath of life to him.'

***

When the boy got bored, like now, his promises of good behaviour were forgotten.

'I'm bloody fed up of this place. It's like the bloody nick. And I'm tired of looking like an Indian in this bloody blanket.' He thought again and then he said: 'And I'm bloody fed up of you and that Western Union Man. You and your silly voice. My Auntie Millie says it's about time you started worrying about your husband, the one you've got now, instead of that other one. That dead one. Dead as a doornail, my Auntie Millie says.'

Della had spent an hour worrying about old Robinette and she had just told herself that she must put her worries out of her mind. With the whole of the American medical profession at his beck and call, with an army of nurses and his Florence Nightingale housekeeper, what could go wrong?'

'Look,' she told the boy. 'I've enough irritations in my life and I don't want to hear another peep out of you. Particularly, I don't want to hear any of the moanings of Menopausal Millie, so just shut up.' He was picking at a loose piece of wool from the Indian blanket. 'And I might just tell you, it isn't just stealing cars and ripping out wires. The way you're going on, you'll be in deep water without any help from machines.'

The boy then said: 'I don't pay any attention to my Auntie Millie, Missus. Honestly I don't.' And he spat on his finger and crossed his chest under the Indian blanket. 'I like you getting them phone calls because they generally put you into a good mood. And them's the only things that does.' And then he mimicked the name, using a strained high pitched voice: 'Eugene, Eugene. Eu——, Eu——, bloody gene. That Eugene, he must have been a ponce with a name like that. Was he, Missus? Was he some kind of a ponce?' And then he walked around the room and he put his hand on the hip of Rixon's pyjamas and minced towards Della, his crooked eyes rolled in what he took to be an imitation of the Eugene he had invented.

'I've had just about enough of you,' Della said and she reached for the telephone again: 'And if it's of any interest to you, I shan't be talking to the Western Union Man this time. I'm ringing Mr Rixon and he can contact your dear Auntie Millie and your Uncle Charlie and they can come and get you.' But she knew that the sight of the ugly boy in the too big striped pyjamas and the Indian blanket camping around the room would have gone straight to Eugene's heart.

The boy tugged at her arm and the blanket fell aside. 'Please, Missus, I'll never say them things again. Don't phone Mr Rixon, Missus.' He had got the buttons of the pyjamas done up wrongly, the holes and the buttons did not coincide and the piece of wool he had pulled in the blanket had made a flaw in it, a newly created weak place where a hole might form. 'And I don't think that Eugene was a ponce. I don't, Missus, honestly.'

She put the blanket over his shoulders again, smoothing it carefully.

'Daniel,' she said. 'It's time you started to do things right.'

Thoughts of old Robinette continued to trouble her. Suppose he really is laid low, she asked herself. That will be a fine state of affairs, the old man sick over there and me snowed in here. But, again, she tried to put the thoughts from her mind. He had had good health and he had taken extravagant care of it, it had obsessed him. His mind had always been full of cures and therapies. Telegrams with warnings about germs and viruses had pursued her from the day she had first met Eugene. Sometimes the messages had been for Eugene only. Take: ENGLAND IN DECLINE STOP IDEA OF MARRIAGE TO ENGLISH GIRL UNWISE STOP TUBERCULOSIS AND SOCIAL DISEASES RAMPANT

IN ALL DEGENERATING NATIONS STOP INSIST BRIDE SUBMITS TO WASSERMAN BEFORE APPROVAL NUPTIALS STOP.

She smiled, remembering her affront at the time.

The old man was so full of shots for this and that, he must by now be resistant to disease. He was riddled with vaccines, preventatives, vitamins and booster shots. The best physicians in the States ministered to his every sneeze. And then, if he really were to fall ill, what was there she could do? At the moment she couldn't even get to the nearest village, let alone to the USA. She sighed and reached for her novel: the lady in the blue car had caught up with the mechanic in the yellow van and he was wiping the black grease from his hands with a white handkerchief. The author was very particular about giving the colour of every object in the book. 'My knees are trembling,' the hero said. *Pink* knees? Did some people really talk to each other like that? Had Eugene ever said to her: 'Della, my knees tremble when I look at you?' Had Tom ever said words like that? 'I feel almost afraid of you,' the man went on, 'and yet I've never been less afraid.' Why that standard of literacy in a grease monkey? I'm not a snob, she reasoned, it's just that if he really is a drop-out graduate, I should have been told. 'And yet, happy as I am, I have a sick feeling that it can't last, something will go wrong.' She looked at the last page to see if it gave any clue. Did he end up dying in a crash or poisoned by carbon monoxide or shot by the wealthy husband? Am I really interested in mechanics with greasy hands who talk too much? she asked herself and put the book aside.

She looked across at the boy: the sight of him surprised her. She had never actually seen him cry before. He held his silent transistor in one hand and he held the Baden-Baden mug close to his face as if it were a receptacle for his tears.

'Daniel,' her voice registered her surprise. 'What's wrong?'

'Mind your own bloody business,' he stammered and choked on the last word.

'Why are you crying?'

'Nothing.' Children always said they cried for nothing.

'Is it because of the snow?'

He shook his head.

'Is it because I said you'd have to go away?' She went to a drawer and took out one of Rixon's handkerchiefs for him.

'It's not because of nothing.'

Lonely? Orphaned? Insecure? No cars to steal? No phones to vandalize?

'If it is because of what I said, I've told you over and over again you don't need to go, if only you'll behave yourself, co-operate. If you'll just be sensible—'

He turned the Baden-Baden mug upside down. She watched but no tears fell from it. He righted it, starting off the strain: 'Uber alles in—'

'And you needn't think I want to stay in this rotten stinking place with you and them lousy cows and horses and them—'

'Sheep,' she supplied the word for him, helping him.

'Uber alles in—' the winding mechanism was running down so that the tune was played too slowly. 'I hate this place and I hate you too.' The boy blew his pink nose loudly on Rixon's pure white handkerchief.

'What about the snow-ploughs,' Rixon asked.

'They haven't been anywhere near.'

'I wonder why we pay our rates.'

'I doubt if they could get up here. They might have been on the main road. I've seen nothing, there's too much drifting.'

'Are you coping with the work all right? The animals?'

'We're having to cope. Daniel will be going out again.'

She heard Rixon cough: 'Look, I'm sorry for my tone earlier on. I didn't realize how bad things were for you up there.'

'I don't think you'll ever make a weather man.'

'No one forecast this.'

'I just don't see you appearing on television with one of those rulers and an atlas. I don't think we'll ever see you manipulating those little symbols of the snow and rain, that's all I mean.'

[83]

'Very, very funny.'

'The postman did say this was coming on. He didn't think it was just a mild flurry. In fact, he warned me that this was how it all began for the poor Thompsons all those years ago.' She looked at the window but saw that it was still packed with snow and there was no hope of seeing auguries in that. 'Anyway, I daresay we shall manage unless things get any worse.'

'Della, don't worry. There isn't any fear of that.'

'I promised that I'd show you Mr Rixon's medal, didn't I?'

She dipped a potato into a bowl of melted snow, peeled it carefully and economically and then washed it clean.

'Old Rixon with a medal for shooting Germans in the back.'

'No, not in the back. Why do you always say such things?' Though truth to tell, some of them must have been wounded in the back. She wiped her hands dry on her apron and then she got the biscuit tin from the cupboard, she opened it and took out the handkerchief in which the purple and silver ribbon was wrapped. A stray earring of hers had got in there too. She fingered the rhinestones, reminiscing.

The boy picked up the medal and examined it and pinned it on to the breast of Rixon's pyjamas which Rixon had never worn. Purple and white against red and black. Left, right, left, right, left, right; he walked his free hand on his knee.

'I've told you to keep that blanket round you.'

'I am. Left, right, left, right, left, right.'

She watched his marching fingers and then she said: 'There was some kind of a hill in Italy. A hill and a bridge, I think. It was cold and muddy. You don't think of it being cold in Italy, but that was what Mr Rixon said.'

When the boy listened carefully, when you hit upon something which really got his attention, his mouth fell open: 'What happened on that hill in all this mud?' He had changed the ribbon over from the pyjamas to the blanket and he began to fire an imaginary rifle: 'Zzzz; kerplunk— kerplunk.'

She waited, counting up to ten. 'Why are you never quiet? If

[84]

you'll shut up for a minute, I'll finish the story. But if you don't want to hear it, just say so.'

His lower lip fell again.

He listened.

'The Germans were trying to move southwards. Sometime Mr Rixon can show it to you on the map. Well, he had got wind of this, he knew that a German convoy was coming through.'

'How did he know?'

'I'm not sure.' How *did* he know? She had never asked him this. She had never introduced Intelligence into any of their conversations, certainly she had never mentioned the word after their reunion because of his jealousy of Eugene. 'I don't know. Maybe someone intercepted a message or got hold of the German plans. Maybe it was radioed to him from H.Q. You can get him to tell you that if he's ever in the mood. Somehow he got news of this convoy and he got his orders too.'

'Someone gave old Rixon orders?'

'Of course, but don't ask me who or—' she introduced the idea carefully, 'it will be feeding up time and I'll never get to the end of the story.' A caravan of young German boys, singing those hateful German songs like the one on the Baden-Baden mug. Young boys, blue eyes, blond hair, coarse like the boy's or light and fine like Hugh's, depending on their quality. She could hear the sound of the trucks and lorries and the sound of the boys' voices singing over them. And every one of them, it came to her, had two fine eyes, two legs, two arms. And every boy in the convoy was some poor mother's son: she quoted her own mother in the war. 'And Mr Rixon crawled out on his stomach to that bridge without any cover such as you'd get here from trees. He had seven sticks of dynamite around him and he crawled and crawled until he reached the bridge.'

The boy's mouth was still open. He was still listening. She had forgotten that the reason she had let him wear Rixon's medal and the reason for telling him the story of Rixon's gallantry was in order to put him in a good mood so that he would make no difficulties about climbing out of the window to go and feed the animals again. Her mind was on the seven sticks of dynamite.

'He put the dynamite in place single-handed.'

'Old Rixon crawling about in the mud.'

'He made sort of mud pies to stick it in. Like children do with flags.'

'Old Rixon making mud pies.'

In those days Rixon's body was as white as snow. And even now it was thin, as thin almost as the boy's. Even now he had no spare flesh. Crawling, wriggling like a snake, no nerves, no sense of fear. Plough your own furrow, carry on. Were all heroes heroes because they could see no danger: because they had no imagination? Didn't heroes see what a stick of dynamite might do to living flesh and living blood and bones? Didn't they see that seven sticks of dynamite might blow their own heads off? Didn't they see that those young German boys with their keen bright eyes might see them first and shoot them down? Were heroes the kind of men who couldn't see that if you neglected a woman ten years younger than you were some nice sensitive American might come into her life and smooth talk her away? Didn't heroes ever see the storms clouds in the sky?

'Is that all?' the boy asked.

'Of course it isn't.'

'Well, go on then.'

'I will, but I don't want any more silly interruptions.'

She watched him fold his arms and clamp his mouth tight shut.

'Now, where was I? Oh yes. Then he crawled all the way back and he had all the men lay down and waited till they heard the convoy.'

'Bang, bang, bang, zing, zing, zing.' The boy unfolded his arms and shot upwards at the Italian sky.

'It's clear you don't want to hear any more.'

'I do, Missus, honestly I do.'

'Mr Rixon and his men put their fingers in their ears and waited.'

[86]

'For what?'

'For the explosion, silly.'

The boy was silent, thinking about it, there were no more words and there was no expression on his face.

'The convoy came into sight at exactly the right time.' Right time for whom? Not for those young German boys. 'Silly boys like you and Hugh.' The timing of the whole operation was perfect, Rixon had told her: perfect. Timing was the only thing that mattered. The fuses went off at the right moment. Synchronized like a ballet, the flame, the tanks, the lorries, the faces on the watches. The most memorable experience of Rixon's life. Rixon, who had always wanted to be a farmer, who had been drafted into the army because his father did not agree to send him to agricultural college, said that medals counted for nothing, it was the beauty of scene that counted. Whizzee, whizzee; bang, bang.

She had not thought about that for a long time. She had not thought about it since she had heard Rixon recounting it to Hugh years and years ago and it had never before occurred to her to wonder if it had been beautiful that day in Pusan when Eugene's body had been blown to pieces by that shell. When Rixon told Hugh about that day in Italy there had been the same look on Hugh's face then as there was on the boy's face now. Hope, expectancy, a desire to hear all about those charred arms and legs. But a soldier's story always stopped at the point where the charge went off and she did not want to think about it any more.

'Go on.'

'That's all.'

'What about them Germans?'

The boy in Rixon's pyjamas and Rixon's medal was excited.

'Did them Germans get fried up?'

Hugh, she thanked God, had grown out of all that now, he was only interested in things of the intellect. War, he said, was undignified. She discovered that she had gripped the rhinestone earring so tightly that the palm of her hand was grazed. Hugh

[87]

said war was reprehensible, it was indefensible, it was a sham. Medals were barbaric. Rixon might as well, he said, wear his victims' teeth around his neck. Why didn't he take up collecting shrunken heads?

'You men, you're all alike, you love shooting and killing. It's like a game.' She put the rhinestone earring down on the table. 'And remember, winning medals isn't everything.'

'Pow, pow, pow,' the boy said, shooting at the opaque window. Then he stopped. 'My dad,' he said and he looked sideways as he formulated one of his wilder lies. 'My dad,' he said and patted the medal on his breast.

Eugene became a soldier as soon as he returned to the States. 'My problem is,' he said, 'I don't like dressing up. I didn't like it at university, I always shunned the carnival and I've always hated clowns. I feel depersonalized in these awful clothes.'

'You look fine to me,' the young Della told him. 'Fine.'

'There isn't much about the army I do like. I don't like the duties, the jargon, anything about it. I feel as if I'm acting in a very badly written play. And I don't think I want to go and kill some poor slant-eyed bastard. Anyway, they'll never trust me with a grenade. They'll put me in some nice warm office checking the laundry lists. Maybe they'll never send me further than D.C.'

Sometimes whole blocks of conversation came back from over the years. Memories revived. Sometimes Eugene's face or voice came into her mind. I've decided, she said to herself, that after this thaws, I'm going to take the old man up on his offer. Tom's established now. He says he can rely on Daniel, well, now's his chance. And Hugh doesn't need *me* any more, he makes that quite clear. Does anyone really need me? Yes, the old man. She decided that she would draw out the bit of money that remained of her legacy. She would buy some clothes, some sunburn lotion and an airline ticket and then she would sail away somewhere with the old man. They would lie out on the sea on rubber floats. They would talk about Eugene. They would rustle up all the old memories from the past, the prizes Eugene got at school, the way he graduated Summa cum Laude, his post-graduate year at Cambridge, the way the old man worried when Eugene wrote to say he had promised himself to an English girl.

Eugene showed her the cablegram from his father: 'I *will* have the blood tests if it worries you,' she'd said.

'Makes no difference, I'd marry you if you had bubonic plague, smallpox, Rocky Mountain Spotted Fever—'

'Leprosy?'

'That too. We're getting married next Tuesday as we planned. We're getting married, come what may. In any case the cable's come a little late. We'd be locking the stable door a little tardily, I'd say.'

Oceans of water had passed under the bridge since then.

'I didn't like the idea of my boy marrying a foreign girl,' the old man said. 'But now I sometimes think that if Eugene hadn't seen you first—' He said this after Eugene was dead.

'Now, Daddy, you must never say such things again. Never, never, never.' Not with poor Eugene's body blown to pieces in a foreign field.

But now she thought: 'That's one thing, old Robinette won't be lusting after me now. *He's* laid low. Besides he always had an eye for youth and beauty, I'm too near to fifty to appeal to him. A lot of years have gone by.'

'Did that Eugene win any medals?' the boy asked, picking up her thoughts again.

'Medals? Good heavens, no.'

'Wasn't he a hero like old Rixon?'

'I'm not sure that I know what a hero is. I'm not sure even that being a hero is a good thing.'

'Was he brave?'

'He was brave enough, but he didn't like war.'

'What did he like then?'

'Eugene? Oh, he liked lots of things. He liked music for one thing. He played the clarinet. He *could* have played in a jazz band. If he'd had time to practise, he was good enough. He

[89]

didn't like the army, but he liked the Phil Silvers Show. He liked a little film star called Nancy Olson. He liked pictures, books, travelling, talking. He liked helping people, doing things.' She found it hard to say exactly what it was that he had liked, just as at this moment with the boy interrogating her, she could not have conjured up the sound of Eugene's voice or the feel of his hands.

'What did he do to help people?'

She tried to think back: 'Well, he was very good to the people who worked for his father. Black people. Things were very hard for black people in those days, they hadn't found their feet. But I think things have improved since then. I remember one of them, an oldish man with toothache. He had to go into hospital to have all of his teeth out. And Eugene paid every penny of that man's hospital bills and his lost earnings. Then he sent him and his wife on a holiday; got new dentures for him, everything. He wouldn't let that man do anything for him in return. He said tears ran down that old man's cheeks when he told him that. All Eugene asked was that the old man and his wife should keep the whole thing secret. Eugene didn't want anyone to know what he'd done.'

Eugene's voice came back to her clearly and she was as startled as if she had really heard a ghost. In spite of Harvard and Cambridge, there had always been that Southern drawl, the long drawn out final syllable: 'When I get out of this God-forsaken place,' he had written, 'I'm going to change sides. I'm going to do something real for the coloured folks.' It was all right to say 'coloured' in those days.

'How did you know then?' the boy asked.

'What?'

'About that man's teeth?'

'Eugene told me, I suppose.'

'I thought he wanted it kept quiet.'

The boy had driven Eugene's voice away. She tried to pursue it, to get it back, the drawl, the 'ah' and 'mah' for 'I' and 'my'. But when a fragment of a voice did come back, it was not

Eugene's voice, it was a voice with English vowels and English intonation. 'Eugene did a lot of things for the underprivileged. That means poor people, in case you didn't know. And he would have done a lot more still when he came out of the army. He *cared* more than any person I've ever known. He planned to practise law; he said he planned to work his fingers to the bone for those people.' *Work my butt off*, Eugene had said.

The boy grinned. 'I don't know why I bother to tell you things, Daniel. You never take anything seriously.'

'I do, Missus. Honestly I do.'

Did he set out to annoy her deliberately or was he just stupid? She looked at him almost secretly, borrowing his own silent style.

'I like hearing about your husbands, honestly I do.'

The plural made her anxious. Was he trying to annoy her again? Looking at his face, it did not seem so. She went into the kitchen and felt at his clothes on the clothes horse. 'Your clothes are drying nicely, but you'd better borrow some of Mr Rixon's to go and feed the animals.' He raised his eyes impatiently and she wondered if he might, after all, refuse to go.

'Just tell me one more thing about Eugene,' he said.

She looked back into the past for something to say about Eugene, something that might be of interest to the boy. 'He had his hair crewcut, quite cropped off. I used to say: "I'll never really know what kind of hair you've got unless you grow it longer." He said that when he got out of the army he'd grow it down to his shoulders if I liked.'

'You never let me grow *my* hair.'

'He never got out of the army though.'

'Was *he* like a film star?'

'You've seen pictures of him, haven't you? He wasn't exactly like a film star, I don't think. But he was good looking.'

The boy bit at his lip.

'Not that I care how a person looks. What matters is what a person has inside. Eugene was kind and he was nice. He liked children, he liked animals.'

The boy was quiet, turning this over in his mind. She congratulated herself: animals! Clever of her to mention them like that. Now the boy might decide to copy Eugene. He might go out and feed the animals without making any more fuss.

'Cat got your tongue?' she asked.

He bit his lip again: 'If that Eugene was good looking like you said—'

'Yes?'

'And if his hair would have been nice if it grew—'

'Of course?'

'Why did he go and marry an ugly old woman like you?'

She answered the telephone, but tried to keep an eye on the television screen, wondering if the interference was due to snow weighing down the lines.

'Mum, take this number, will you? I've only got ten pence.'

'You know your father gets angry about the bills.'

'Mother, hurry.'

She searched for a pencil.

'I've left a book behind,' Hugh said. The snow had tampered with the telephone as well. 'Can you send it on?'

Stamps, sellotape, brown paper, string.

'Today, if you can.'

The pips began to sound, she dialled the number he had given her and she heard him on the line: 'Hugh, I can't send it today. We're snowed in. The only way we can get out of the house at all is by climbing out of the window, the bedroom window at that. Your father's had to stay at Grandma's, he's sleeping on the bed settee. He just can't get home at all, he says.' There was a severe crackling on the line. She shook the receiver.

'Mo*ther*.' He had a way of accentuating the last syllable too, but *his* way meant that she was a fool. She shouted for the boy:

[92]

'Daniel, look in Hugh's bedroom, will you. See if you can find his book.'

'What kind of book?'

'Hang on, I'll ask. What kind of book?' she said to Hugh.

'For Heaven's sake: a book.'

'For Heaven's sake,' she shouted up, 'a book.'

'Why do *I* have to do everything?' the boy asked.

'Hugh, we're completely cut off here. Haven't you seen anything on the news? There's terrible drifting and there's still a blizzard blowing.' More crackling on the line.

'That's terrible. I don't know why you ever bought that damned place.'

She formed the words: 'Don't worry about me, will you?' to reassure him about her safety in the storm.

'I've simply got to have that book.'

The boy came downstairs, dressed for going out. He held the book by one cover. A letter fell from it and fluttered to the floor. She remembered the other letter.

'Oh, by the way, a letter came just after you'd gone.'

'Why the bloody hell didn't you forward it?'

'The snow.'

'Why didn't you give it back to the postman?'

'It didn't seem necessary at the time. Shall I open it and read it to you?'

'Not on your Nellie. Can't I have any privacy?'

'As you like.'

'And please send that book on.'

'I'll ring for a helicab,' she said. 'And remember, dear, get some change next time before you ring.'

'For Christ's sake, Mother, sometimes I wonder if you want to hear from me at all.'

The boy said that he wasn't going out to feed old Rixon's rotten animals in rotten weather like this unless he could keep the rotten medal on. He had pinned it to Rixon's duffle coat which he had borrowed.

[93]

Della said that she did not think that that was a good idea because it might get lost outside. The boy stuck out his lower lip again. Then Della said he *could* wear the medal if it meant so much to him. After all, what did a bit of ribbon matter? Thoughts like that were disloyal to Rixon who had risked his life fighting for his country. But the medal had been purchased with the blood of those poor German boys and so she need not feel guilty about using it as a bribe. The boy breathed on the ribbon on the duffle coat. Breathing on ribbon? What point was there in that?

'My dad got *two* medals for killing Germans in the war.'

'I daresay.'

'Better medals than old Rixon too.'

'The Victoria Cross, you mean?'

'Is that the best? What you just said?'

He started towards the bedroom stairs, walking tall because he had the medal on. Della followed, reminding him of the signals they had agreed. 'No more snowmen. The sun is going down and I want you back in soon. Pronto.'

'I know, I know, I know.' Walking behind him, she heard these words, dismissing her.

He sat on the window-sill and he swung his legs over. 'None of your tomfoolery this time, Daniel, please.' She leaned out of the window to watch him go, but before he was out of sight, she thought of his father and the Victoria Cross and she wanted to call after him to remind him that he had once told her that his father had not been able to get into the army because of his weak chest. But what did it matter what kind of uniform your father wore: khaki, arrow-patterned, navy blue. None of that mattered when the chips were down and you were stuck here in this snow.

More of it was coming down: I think I'm beginning to be frightened, she thought. She was aware that this was the first time she had let this come into her head.

'She must have gone deaf,' he told the snowman. 'She's supposed to shout back every time I shout.' This idea which he had just invented surprised him. 'Old Della deaf? So what's the point of me wasting my breath?'

He did not go into the bull's shed immediately and considered not going in there at all. It could wait till morning. He might have felt lonely out here on his own in the snow, but he did not see the portents Della saw in the yellow sky. He spun himself around and around to see the disturbance his feet had made in the top layer of the snow. Here and there was a bare patch where a bit of vegetation thrust up free from snow and ice. He plucked a straw and sucked it in his mouth, pretending it was a cigarette.

There was something wrong with the bull. It coughed a wracking cough. He went up close to it, ignoring Della's warnings. He saw that its eyes were reddened and inflamed. He had had a bad cold himself in the autumn and Della had got a bottle of medicine for him; he recalled its pleasant taste.

He cleaned out the shed, not thinking about danger from the bull and not locking the door as he went in and out. The animal did not look at him and it did not touch the food and water he had put out for it. It stood still, coughing its cough. He cupped water in his two hands and held it out to the bull, meeting it square on. He was nearer to it than he had ever been to any bull, close to its hot breath and its burning eyes. The bull turned away from him, not touching the water in his hands. He let them fall. A slight sense of worry about the animal troubled him, but putting it aside he left the shed, shaking his head from side to side.

When he watched television, he participated, riding bucking broncos on his chair, firing shots at bandits, dancing to waltzes and singing to ragtime tunes.

'Supper's ready, Daniel. Come on.'

'No, you come here, Missus, watch this.'

She stood at the entrance to the kitchen, sipping sherry, one of the few luxuries left since the snow. The screen heroine in tight-waisted gingham toted a gun. Her lips too were tight as she looked at her husband.

'You're a gal who never has a smile on her face,' he told her.

'A woman who gets hitched up to a man like you can't find much to smile about,' she told him. The man, Della gathered, was the kind who always came the long way home. He kept the sociable side of his nature for the girls at the saloon.

'Why does this drivel appeal to you?' she asked the boy.

He waved a hand, signalling her to be quiet.

A younger man sat in the corner of the cabin, chipping a piece of wood with a knife: 'If I kin ever be of any help, ma'am,' he told the heroine.

'Help? I don't need any of that from any man,' the heroine said through her clenched lips.

'No one ever offers me any help,' Della said. 'Maybe if I got a gingham dress or even a gun.'

'Sh—' the boy said.

The hero then explained that he was gonna ride out West and the heroine gestured to him with her gun, holding the barrel a little too close to his head for Della's liking. Tears trickled down the heroine's cheek. The boy told Della that the tears weren't real, they were made of glycerine.

'Your technical knowledge stuns me,' Della said and again he told her to be quiet and that it was bad enough having to watch this picture in black and white without her talking all the time and then he began to ride the Windsor chair violently as if it were the hero's horse.

'You watch that chair. If you break it, I'll deduct it from your wage and you still owe me for that jug last week. You'll be paying me back until the summer and that's only supposing you don't break anything else, which is unlikely the way you rampage about.'

'I shan't be here in the summer, I shall go to America and be a cowboy.'

'You don't like cows.'

'What's that got to do with it?' He sat still on the chair.

'Only that cowboys take care of cows.'

'Not me. I'll take care of something else. Horses?'

'There are horses here, but I've never noticed you rushing out to take care of them.'

'I mean *real* horses; not those creepy things of yours.' He looked straight at her. 'My Uncle Charlie says they're only good for glue.'

She drained her glass: 'Well, supposing you got to America? What makes you think anybody would want to take you on?'

'I'll ride in rodeos.'

'You've never even been on a horse.'

'I'm going to when the snow goes.'

'Not on *my* horses.'

'I'll find a horse somewhere.'

'Steal one, you mean. It'll make a nice change from cars.'

He looked round, smiling, secret, shy: 'Missus, don't say that. You know I've given up pinching cars.'

'That reminds me, tomorrow's your social worker's day.'

'Bugger.'

'Don't let me hear you say that word again.'

The heroine cooked hominy grits for the young man. The young man rode his chair just like the boy. 'Looks like you're not happy, ma'am,' he said. The heroine poked at the grits.

It occurred to Della to wonder how the heroine ever got a husband with that sulky face. She was no beauty. With a face like that why did that young man adore her so?

Meantime the hero had called into the saloon for a last look at the girls in their frilly knickers. After a time, he tore out of the saloon and jumped on to his horse and set off for the West.

'Why did he run out like that?' the boy asked.

'I don't know.'

'Where is he going to?'

'You've been watching the film. How is it that you sit with

your nose on the screen all night and then you ask me what the picture is about?'

'Don't *you* know why he's going off then?'

'Since when did I understand anything about men? Maybe he doesn't like hard manual work. Maybe he thinks he has better things to do than sticking round at the ranch taking care of the animals. Maybe he feels that's woman's work. Maybe he feels that buying the place and stocking it up with useless animals is the sole extent of his responsibility.'

The boy sat stock still in his chair. He had not yet told Della about the bull and its cough and if he did tell her now she might make him go out in the dark to check on it.

On television the sun set in the golden West.

'Come on, Daniel, eat your hominy before it gets any colder. Then we'll have an early night so you can dream about being a cowboy,' Della said.

It would be wrong to read the letter, but she read it anyway. It was in Hugh's handwriting and addressed to 'Bee'. 'This bloody place,' the letter said. 'Imagine a set for one of those old time movies, starring Bela Lugosi, maybe. Walls two feet thick. (The old man mentions that with pride as if a lot is expected of me because of it.) My mother and I seem to be trapped in some World War II dream of his. Foxhole Fantasies or Dreams in a Piggy Bank.

'Believe me I can't wait to get back to your little urban house so I can shake off the rubble and the rocks.

'I feel as if I'm deserting Mum. She's changed a lot, looks at herself in the mirror constantly, though I don't think she knows she's doing it. I think she's looking for the little girl who caught the rich American all those years ago. Hard to think that he and my dad practically fought a duel for her at the altar. I don't think my old man would do much fighting for her now.'

The blue ink smudged. The paper had got damp. She dried it by the fire, putting it so close to the flame that steam rose from it. She smoothed it out, treating it with the deference with

[98]

which she treated all of Hugh's possessions. The paper scorched a little. She drew in her breath and then to her own surprise she screwed it up and flung it on the fire. The blue ink persisted strangely as the paper went up in flames against the dying coals.

❖❖❖

The boy woke up in the night and screamed. He had dreamed that the ceiling was coming in and crushing him to death. In addition, in his dream the damp walls of the house were caving in. Della woke up and went in to his bedroom and she saw that the boy was clutching at his throat as if tearing off the hands of an assailant who was strangling him.

'The ceiling's coming in.'

'The ceiling?' She looked up. 'Don't be silly, you've been dreaming. Hugh's ceiling is very damp, but there's nothing wrong with yours.'

'It *could* come in with all that snow on top of it.'

She tried to laugh. 'It might, but there isn't really any sign of it at all. That roof has held up for one hundred years, it must have seen weather like this often enough. Roofs were built properly in those days.'

But she did not tell him that when she had gone in to Hugh's room that night to turn the cat out of it, the same fear about the ceilings had come into her mind. This was the oldest part of the house, this had been the Monks' Look Out all those years ago. But did its antiquity really make it less vulnerable or did it make it more so? 'A strong roof like that won't ever come down. You're thinking about the roofs on the new houses they're putting up. This roof is made of oak; it'd take more than a bit of snow and a puff of wind—' She looked at the beams, they were riddled with woodworm and dry rot.

'Looks to me as if the ceiling's coming in.'

'Solid oak—' she reached up and knocked at the beam: 'Safe as houses.' She tried to reassure herself with her words. 'You've

[99]

had a bad dream. You've too much imagination. You're just like Hugh, he used to have dreadful nightmares.'

'About the ceiling coming in?'

'We didn't live here then. We used to live in the South. We had a nice little semi just near the bank. Hugh used to get frightened on his own, he was frightened of the dark. Every shadow used to terrify him. When his father was away he used to come and sleep in my room with me.' There was a large, strong cobweb in the corner but nowadays they said that you should leave cobwebs alone because of the ecology. In her fatigued state she began to enter into the boy's dream, she would not be able to move the cobweb lest it disturb the balance of the delicate ceiling. When the snow went there would be a lot of cleaning up to do, the cobweb could wait till then.

There had been another element in the boy's dream which had troubled him and now it came into his conscious mind. In his dream the bull had been crushed to death under an avalanche of snow, but he did not dare mention this to Della. He went on holding himself together with his arms and then he said: 'Missus, can I come and sleep in your room?'

'Daniel. What will you think up next?'

'Like you said Hugh used to.'

The body of a forgotten bluebottle decayed in the dusty web.

'Hugh was just a little boy.'

This boy was nearly six feet tall. Down sprouted from his upper lip and his voice was deep. But sitting up in bed, wearing pyjamas meant for a man, he looked like a child. A child to whom she owed something, though what the debt was she could not decide. He bit his lip. He was thinking hard or maybe biting back his tears.

'And you see Daniel, even if the roof did fall in, it would fall in in my room too, so you wouldn't be any better off in there, would you? I really don't know why we're discussing such things. There is absolutely no danger, we had the roof reinforced the year we came in here.' She pulled her dressing gown round her as she started out of the room.

[100]

'You'd let Hugh sleep with you, wouldn't you? And he's a lot older than me,' she heard him calling after her as she went out of the room.

'ENTERO VIOFORM EXCELLENT FOR COMBATING SUMMER DIARRHOEA STOP. Shall I read out the exact dosage? I've got it here?'

'Sorry, I've had an awful night. The boy woke me up, he'd got it into his head that the ceiling was coming in. I'm not really wide awake yet. I'm not quite sure that I've taken in what you were saying. It was *Summer* Diarrhoea?'

'That's what's written here.'

'It sounds odd.'

'Do you want me to query it?'

'Don't bother, it won't do me any harm to look ahead for once. It won't always be winter, will it? Blue skies are probably just around the corner. It's probably rather sunny where *he* is. I don't think I'll worry about the dosage though. It's only January. However, if it makes you happy to recommend cures for Summer Diarrhoea, I don't mind.'

'I don't compose the messages, I only transmit them.'

'I realize that. You're not the kind of man who'd warn me about mosquito bites on Christmas Eve.'

'I didn't even transmit that one. I had Christmas Eve off.'

'I'd forgotten that, it seems so long since Christmas, doesn't it?'

'Time flies.'

'I don't even know what day it is.'

'Wednesday. The other man has every Wednesday off. Tuesday night is his choir practice night, he needs Wednesday off to recover from the low notes. Did you notice that deep baritone when he suggested dosing yourself with quinine? He tries it out on the customers to keep himself in voice.' Sometimes when he talked she sat back to listen. 'Funny to think of you snowed in there, because it's very beautiful here, there's even a bird on the window-sill.'

'Carrier pigeon?'

'No, a starling, I think. Or are they all in Africa?'

'Poison its birdseed. It's probably in the pay of a foreign power, trained to crack the code. It'll be turning "Summer Diarrhoea" over in its birdbrain even now.'

'There's more here for it to work on. He's sent a bumper crop today.'

'Poor old man, he must have had a sleepless night. Read them, will you? I'm eager for contact with the big world outside this farm.'

'Here goes: TOTAL BEDREST ORDERED BECAUSE OF FEVERISH COLD STOP UP TO ONE HUNDRED AND TWO. I think that must be his temperature, do you? Then there's another "Stop". He's lavish with them today: Wall Street must have gone up in sympathy. TRIP TO CARIBBEAN NOW IMPERATIVE FOR HEALTH REASONS STOP SURVIVAL MAY DEPEND ON IT STOP CABLE IMMEDIATELY. He means business now.'

'I suppose I *must* let him know one way or the other.'

'Sounds as if the time has come.'

'I suppose I'll have to say no. Pity, I don't like to think of the old man laid low with no family around.'

'Say yes then.'

'It's not as easy as all that.'

'You mean your husband doesn't want you gallivanting around the world'.

'He says he doesn't mind. But I don't really see how I can be spared. He insists that he and the boy have got the whole thing in control, but I don't know. Besides if I *go* I don't think I'd have the heart to come back. I think that a taste of that Caribbean luxury would be too much for me. In any case, I'm a prisoner in the snow.'

'If I were your husband—' the Western Union Man said and she could hear a slight whistling on the line. The bird on the window-sill? 'I'd not take kindly to your getting invitations to run off with rich old men. I'd put a stop to it, I'd tell him he's not your father-in-law now. But then I'm an old-fashioned type of man.'

[102]

'My husband is old-fashioned too.'

'Doesn't he mind you being exposed to temptation?'

'Temptation on the telephone?'

'It won't be on the telephone once you get to the Caribbean.'

'I don't think my husband sees me as the kind of woman who'd attract another man. Not any longer. He seems to think that Robinette's interest is some kind of joke, the cablegrams amuse him.'

'They amuse me, but I don't think they're a joke. I think he's not yet realized you aren't still his daughter and he sounds like a man who is used to getting his own way. No matter how long it takes. But I'd better get on and read the other cables or you won't be getting your money's worth from me. This is a nice one: FEARS FOR YOUR FEET RENEWED STOP COMPLICATIONS FROM CHILBLAINS MAY LEAD TO AMPUTATION OF FEET OR WORSE.'

'What is worse than the amputation of the feet?'

'REMEMBER WELL EPIDEMIC WORLD WAR I STOP BEWARE RUBBING IN SNOW AS ADVOCATED ARMY MANUAL NINETEEN SEVENTEEN STOP OLD REMEDIES OFTEN DUBIOUS STOP PATENT CURE SUGGESTED STOP NAME SLIPS MIND STOP WILL CABLE SEPARATELY WHEN IT RETURNS.'

'Another false hit; even in *this* cold place, I'm free of chilblains. In fact, for a woman of forty-eight, I'm not in bad condition when you consider the strangely difficult life I have to lead. Sometimes I have a painful ache in my side. But he never seems able to dream up a cure for that.'

'Well today it seems to me that when you've said chilblains and Summer Diarrhoea you've said everything so far as *your* health is concerned. Today it's *his* health he's worrying about. BRONCHITIS PLAGUED BY TIRESOME COUGH STOP MEDICAL ADVISOR INSISTS SLEEP REGIME STOP FOLLOWED BY STAY IN ADVANTAGEOUS CLIME STOP CONGENIAL CONCERNED COMPANY ESSENTIAL TO WELL BEING STOP AS DAUGHTER AND ONLY LIVING RELATIVE HOPE SEE DUTY CLEAR.'

There was a pause.

'You see what I mean,' the man said. 'He's not going to listen to No this time.'

'I'm beginning to wonder if I can *say* No this time. Bronchitis, he's never had that before. There's a real ring of truth in it. He's had the odd illness over the years, but it's always been expensive things like oyster poisoning, colitis, gout. The idea that he has a real illness with a name that I can recognize quite frightens me.'

'Maybe he's blackmailing you.'

'Not with bronchitis: for blackmail he'd choose cholera or Tsu tsu gamushi disease, something with zing.' She thought about the old man for a moment and then she said: 'He's in his late seventies, you know; bronchitis could turn serious. Is there anything else in the cable?'

'That one ends: POSITION CRITICAL STOP COME TO MY SIDE FOR EUGENE'S SAKE IF NOT FOR MINE. And there is a prepaid cable if you want to send an answer back.'

'Let me think,' Della said and her mind turned to Rixon and then it turned to Hugh; her husband and her son, neither of them seemed to need her. Hugh had his Bee (Beatrice?); Rixon had his bull. To each his own. 'Okay,' she said at last. 'As soon as there's a thaw, I'm going. Pronto. Cable him, will you please? Tell him I'm snowed in. Tell him I'm a captive in this goddam place. Tell him I'll get a visa and fly to his bedside or, if he can make it, to the Caribbean. I'll join him immediately anywhere I can with a British passport. And tell him that once I get there, I'll be staying for a long long time.' Her words spilled out. 'And if there are enough words left over, tell him that I was crazy ever to leave him in the first place, I should have listened to him when he tried to talk me out of marrying Tom. I should have believed him when he said that marriage and motherhood were overrated. Tell him I could have saved myself a lot of trouble, if I'd stayed where I was.'

'Hold on, hold on,' the man said. 'I'm having difficulty taking all this down.'

'Don't worry. Here's an opportunity to do a little composing of your own. I don't care how you put it, but tell him I'm worried about the bronchitis and I'll be over there to take care of him as soon as the thaw comes.'

The man hesitated and then he said: 'You mean you're going to burn your boats?'

'That's right. I am. I'm going to undo all the harm I've done myself.'

'Leaving hearth and home?'

Della looked around the little room as if she were a stranger looking at it for the very first time: small, damp, thick-walled, white.

'Believe me, I shan't be leaving very much behind.'

From her bedroom window she saw that more snow was falling. Well, what did it matter? It couldn't last for ever and soon she'd be going back to a life no one with any brains would ever have left, a life where she was prized and needed. She would go straight to Mimosa Street if the old man was too sick to move and if she could get a visa, or she would fly to some warm island and negotiate a visa from there. It came to her that she might not miss her husband and son at all. What insane biological urge had led her to fly back to marry Rixon? That urge was one of the attributes of youth, the stuff that the survival of the species is made of. And now that the word 'survive' had entered her mind, she began to admit, a little sadly, that there might be some doubt about survival for her and the boy.

He came up behind her, carrying one of his wellingtons in his hand. 'My Uncle Charlie says that you don't treat me right.'

'Your Uncle Charlie?' For a moment she had to think hard to remember who he was talking about. 'Have you been on the telephone to him during the night? Waking your Auntie Millie from her beauty sleep?'

He was in one of his annoying moods again but she would not be exposed to them for long. She would remain cheerful, because one way or another it was all coming to an end. 'What is your Uncle Charlie complaining about now?'

'Sending me out in the snow and making me sleep in that cold room with no proper roof on.'

'Doesn't conform to the Factories Act. I'll put it to Mr Rixon, if he ever drops in again.'

She noticed an enlarged vein in her leg, something ugly and ungainly. She rubbed at it, wondering if it were varicosed and, if it were, why she had never noticed it before. If the roof was giving way, as the boy said, a vein would be the least of her troubles, so there was a silver lining to every cloud. And if the roof didn't fall in, there'd be the aeroplane ride and old Robinette would recover immediately. She and the vein would give him a reason to go on living.

'He said he could report you to the cruelty people.'

'Not to mention the Minister of Works.' It *was* a varicose vein. 'Tell me, when did your Uncle Charlie say all this, Daniel?'

'Mmm?'

'When did you talk to him?'

'He said it,' his tongue protruded from his mouth as he searched his mind and the hand holding the wellington boot rubbed at his head, 'yesterday. I told him all the things you make me do and he said he'd have something to say to you.'

'Ah well, if you'd been listening to me talking on the telephone just now, you'd realize that I'm not going to be here to make you do anything for much longer.'

He looked at her with his sideways look. She thought of telling him that a flying doctor had phoned to tell her that she had an incurable condition and that the boy might have to get a spade and bury her in the snow. 'You going somewhere, Missus?' the boy asked and his face was frightened.

'That's one telephone call you've missed.'

'I've been looking for my other wellington, Missus.'

An invasion by a one-legged man?

She smiled: 'It didn't occur to you that it might be *me* who ran away to America to ride in the rodeo, did it?'

'Are you going to that old man?'

'My father by marriage? Why not?'

'What will old Rixon do?'

'He manages very nicely without me. Anyway, you said *you* were his manager; *you're* in charge.'

The boy placed the solitary wellington boot down on the floor. 'You can't leave Hugh.'

'Hugh? Hugh doesn't need a mother any more. He's not had much time for me since he was thirteen.'

'Will you really ride in the rodeo?'

'Why not? I had a fine seat in my day, or so they said. And when I get my varicose vein attended to, there will be no holding me.'

The boy kicked at the wellington boot with his slippered right foot. 'Missus,' he said, 'what about me?'

'You?'

'What will happen to me when you've gone?'

'I should have thought you'd have been delighted to get rid of me. You're always telling me you're sick of me. Just think what a life you'll have with me out of the way. No one to shout at you; no one to tell you what to do. You can get up when you like; only work when the mood takes you; play the transistor as loud as it will go. There'll be nobody here who gives a damn.'

The boy was quiet and then he came up with an idea: 'Missus, can I come with you when you go?'

'What a wonderful idea.'

'I could help you, keep you company, things like that.'

'That,' said Della, 'is all I need.'

'You mean I can come?'

'The main reason I'm going is to get away from you. You and that bloody bull. Anyone who has had to spend any time with you deserves a bit of peace. Peace and pleasure and luxury, that's what I'm looking for. I've had enough of being a prisoner and a slave. I'm going where I'll be appreciated.'

'The old man is crazy about you,' Eugene once said.

'You think everyone is crazy about me.'

'It's those long legs. I had to stop him from taking up with a showgirl once. She had a face like a horse and a voice like a horse, but he never looked further than her legs.' Eugene was changing out of his uniform when he told her that, he was putting on a sharp new suit. 'But with you, it's not just legs, its face and hair and all of you—'

'If he's as crazy about me as you say he is, why was he so opposed to the idea of you marrying me?'

'He likes everything to be *his* idea. And then, he has a strong sense of property. He doesn't like anyone muscling in on his territory.' She thought about this now; did all men like property? 'You see,' Eugene went on to say, 'the old man and I have been pretty close since Mother died. Pretty damn close.' He was looking into the mirror as he tied his tie and she could see her own figure in the glass and then Eugene turned around to look at her and he had to shade his eyes because she was standing in the sun: 'The old man and I were sort of thrown together and so, I guess, the idea of my taking anyone else on board was not very welcome.'

'So he lost his showgirl, but you gained me.'

'Could I have let him marry a woman with a face like that?'

'I don't think you should have interfered,' she'd said. 'After all, she had those legs and maybe other qualities you didn't even know about.'

Eugene could never tie a tie; take that day, for instance. He had stood and looked at her, his blue eyes slanted against the Southern sun, with his fingers becoming impatient with the tie. She remembered that he had flung it aside.

'Missus,' the boy said to her from the window, calling her back to the present time.

'Yes, what now?'

'I need some cough medicine for the bull.'

'What on earth do you mean?'

'I think it's got flu.'

'Flu? Why do you say that?'

'Coughing and coughing all the time. It wouldn't eat or drink a thing.'

'And you've waited to tell me until *now?*'

'I forgot.' His eyes, like the remembered Eugene's eyes, were almost closed, as if the world had begun to dazzle him. 'And, anyhow, you don't like that bull. So I can't see why you care whether it's got a cough or not.'

'Like it? What the hell has that got to do with it? Useless as it is, it's the most expensive animal on this farm.' She shook her hands helplessly. 'And apart from that, I don't like any of the animals to suffer, you know that.'

'Well,' the boy said and he began to pull the single wellington on his foot, 'just give me the cough mixture and I'll go. I'll soon make it better with a spoonful of that.'

'Oh no you won't, you're not going out again. You can ring your Uncle Charlie and tell him that from now on we're changing places, you and me. I'll climb out of the window and you can do all the work inside. You can start by cooking that bacon and making the toast and coffee.' He stabbed at the rind with a kitchen knife, unravelling it from the fat. His look was speculative.

'You're going to climb out of the window, Missus? You're going to slide down the snow?'

'Why not? I'll know everything's done properly if I do it myself and I won't have to worry about you fooling about. I couldn't make as much of a pig's ear of things as you do, if I tried.' She watched him lick the grease from his fingers one by one. 'If I could just see the reason why you didn't bother to tell me about that bull—' The tips of his fingers were all in his mouth and she could not tell whether the gesture was due to worry or reverie. She went out of the kitchen to check on the sodden blankets which wedged the door. She wondered why she had ever thought that blankets would be any use. Her leg had begun to hurt at the site where she had discovered the enlarged vein. But she told herself that this was nonsense: why should it only start to hurt today, coincident with her realization that it was there? Real pain would have manifested itself before. 'And I shall want this whole place cleaning up. Wash up the pots and vacuum all the floors. Upstairs and down, the electricity's still on.' The top of her wellingtons caught on the vein. She looked down at the boots, detesting them. And then she thought of the shoes she had worn when she was young: pointed toes, stiletto heels, shoes with ankle straps. Well, what the hell, when the thaw came she would go and live with Robinette and he would find a cure all for her many ills: FOR MIDDLE AGED LADIES WORN OUT BY LIFE SUGGEST— And Rixon and the boy could live here together forever like pigs in clover and Hugh could stay with his spires and his secret Bee.

'And don't forget, as soon as you've finished the housework ring up your bloody Uncle Charlie and tell him that there'll be changes as soon as all this goes,' and she waved a hand at the intruding snow. 'When it goes, I go too. Tell him he'll have to find someone else to complain about, because I'll be in some Hilton Hotel close to the deep, blue sea. And from the time my new shoes sink into the pile of that carpet, I'll do any complaining there is to do. Let there be one wrinkle in my sheet and I'm telling you, they'll hear from me. If the Whisky Sours aren't iced to my taste, then, wow, they'll see the feathers fly. I've had enough of cold, privation and this place. I've had enough of Rixon's Folly and I've had enough of you.'

Whilst he waited he did not clean the house up as she had said and he did not ring his Uncle Charlie either; instead he felt down the edges of the sofa. Sofas sometimes yielded riches; pennies, ball point pens and once an antique brooch, a brooch Della had lost a long time ago. Della had been very pleased with him that day and she said that she had searched everywhere for that brooch and she had been very worried about it because it belonged to her grandma and she had said that she would always be grateful to him for finding it: very, very grateful. She had gone on being grateful for over a week. He had pricked his hand quite badly when he found the brooch and Della had seen him sucking the blood. She had taken his hand in hers, one of the few times she had ever touched him, and then she had washed his hand with warm water and then put Dettol on the wound.

'I don't mind getting my hand pricked again,' he told the cat.

He prayed that he could find another brooch, a ring, a string of pearls, or better still an earring to match the one which Della had found in the biscuit tin. If he could find something nice, she might forget what he said his Uncle Charlie had said, might forgive him for not telling her about the bull. He kneeled down by the side of the sofa and moved the cushions to give himself more scope. His hands moved rapidly from side to side.

'Please God, let me find something for her. A present, something nice. Please God, put something there, so that the Missus won't go away.'

The moment she stepped out of the window, the boy went out of her thoughts. Though she had feared the climb out of the window, the cold air cleared her mind. The slight stiffness in her joints which she suffered made the going hard. Usually she was afraid of heights, but the fear seemed to be in abeyance because the white snow levelled the landscape. There were some patches of green, patches from which the snow had blown away and sometimes there were grey-green patches on the old walls at the side of the house. The journey she was embarking on was like a sporting event, as if the climb down the snowbank was just the first part of an obstacle race, a Winter Olympic.

Somehow she found herself thinking of the men she had married: What would they think of me just now? The hill in Italy and the tank in Korea came back to her. Eugene and Tom would think nothing of this slide down the snow. The faces of the two men merged as so often happened; they became one, their voices intermingled so that she could not separate them. She closed her eyes and slid and when her feet reached the ground she looked up at the sky with resignation. The sky was heavy with snow but from the outside of the house this seemed to be of less significance than from the inside. She stood up and looked at the roof and, seeing it, she realized that the boy's fears were not unreasonable, the volume of snow on the rooftop might be a real cause for alarm. There would be no hope of escape if the building collapsed. But did old buildings collapse unless there was an earthquake or volcanic eruption? And who could she get to authorize Air Sea Rescue? 'I have a bull with a cough and there's a lot of snow on my roof.' No, the only hope of escape would be a cable to Robinette, tell him: 'Send helicopter, airlift me. Stop. Boy, Stop. Bull. Stop. Cows, Stop. Sheep, Stop. Horses.' She hesitated for a moment. 'Yes, Stop. Dogs, Stop. Cat.' Up in the sky she saw some kind of aeroplane, circling around the moors. Maybe old Robinette had sent it, she looked for a message, some trail of vapour to indicate that rescue was at hand: DO NOT DESPAIR DAUGHTER STOP SALVATION ORGANIZED. She described these letters in the air with her finger. then, slowly, she let her hand fall.

She stood still, straight, orientating her body in the falling snow. She felt like one of those men on the moon, trying to learn to walk upright. This world was like the moon, colourless except for those freak areas of green.

At the door of the cowhouse she stopped. The bottom of it was submerged in snow. Had the boy been lying when he said he'd fed the animals? It looked as if this door hadn't been opened. Or had this snow fallen more recently? She bent down and scratched with her hands, she was becoming afraid of what she would find inside the door. If the boy had been lying, she might find a graveyard in the shed. But when the door opened at last, the lame cow greeted her with something like recognition and the other cows looked at her with their dark eyes. She put a hand out to the lame cow and it rubbed against her. 'As soon as the snow goes,' she said, 'I'll be leaving here, I'll be going back where I belong.' A slight tightness came into her throat. 'But don't you girls worry about that. Tom will take care of you. He thinks a lot more about you and that bull than he's ever thought of me. He'll see that you're all right.' She patted the cow again and then she set to and cleaned out the whole of the cowhouse, not noticing how hard the work was until she had stopped. She laid more straw and then she filled up the food and water troughs. 'It'll soon be over,' she said. 'Weather like this never lasts very long. Then Tom will come home and the first thing he'll do is come tearing in here to see that you're all right. I'll guarantee that *will* be the first thing he'll do, or, come to think of it, the second. First he'll visit Moby Dick.'

Whenever she opened the door of the bull's shed, she found her heart beating rapidly, not just from fear but from suppressed disgust. The bull was the only animal she could not talk to. Bulls did not listen as other animals did. The door of the shed swung badly. The thought came to her that the boy might have left the bull untethered or he might have tormented it so that she might be in danger. She listened but there was no sound from the bull. A new wind was getting up so that she might not have heard a sound from inside the door even if there had been one.

She dragged at the door and then she heard that there *was* some kind of a noise, some kind of a cough. It sounded as if someone, someone human, had by a miracle made his way from the village to the farm and had chosen to lie in wait for her by the barn. There were no footprints to indicate this. Footprints in the snow could soon be covered over, even the boy's were covered over now. The bull was standing, its head turned slightly towards her, but it did not seem to see her with its red eyes, weary and inflamed by infection. Its cough seemed as if it might strangle it. The food the boy had left for it was almost untouched. The animal seemed to have diminished in size. Where was the big animal she and Tom had tended? Was that yesterday or the day before? She went towards it. She saw the veins pulsating in its great neck; each cough sent a shudder through it. Saliva dripped from its nose and mouth and straw stuck to its face. Then its gross body and its huge cruel head with its stupid, weary look came nearer to her; she did not move away as she would have done two days ago. Her arm moved and touched its ringed nose very gently so that her skin came into contact with the hot, dry flesh. Then for the first time ever the bull looked straight into her eyes. And at that time it came back to her who the maiden in mythology was: Europa, the young girl who fell in love with the white bull. 'Moby, I don't think you're the stuff that myths are made of.' She cupped her hands to bring water to it, but it did not seem able to drink, and so she cooled its nose with the water, not wanting to waste it. A little anger rose in her: 'You realize, Moby, I *told* Tom that if he insisted on buying you then he must take all the responsibility for you. I said that on no account was I to be left alone with you. And look at me, the very first crisis and here I am. It isn't even as if I liked you. I don't. I don't like any bulls. Not ugly, shapeless, black ones. Why am I in here? I'm not happy about it. I've always been afraid of you and I would be now if I had any sense.' Her wet hand went of its own accord to soothe the animal's heaving throat. The bull coughed: its heavy eyes fixed on her. 'So don't go getting dependent on me, will you? Because my days here are numbered.' She went to the rotten creaking rusted door and collected a large handful of snow and eased it down the bull's throat very gently. 'That's right, cool liquid will make it better. I'll go and get some medicine for you. You'll soon be better. I might get a vet. Daniel said they might fly one in. Why not? You've got a pedigree, you've got blue blood. People will do anything for sick animals. So don't worry.' She tried once more to get the bull to drink, but it could not and its painful cough followed her all the way out of the shed.

The sheep seemed to be defeated by the snow. She walked past mounds which suggested to her that victims had been claimed already. She must get a spade after she had attended to the bull, she must see if she could dig some of them out, save them if there was a chance. They said that sheep could live for days under the snow, but was that right? Or was that just a myth too? One sheep at least was dead, she saw its still feet protruding from a heap of snow, they were together, placed neatly as if they had been arranged tidily for death. The horses were the only sign of hope, they had trotted around in a circle in the snow: a perfect circle. Their instinct had told them to keep moving to keep their circulation going and to keep a pathway open. A pathway which they and some of the sheep could use for access to their food. Two of the horses were in foal and several of the sheep were due to lamb because Rixon had chosen this year to experiment, to stagger the breeding season. Why had he done it *this* year? To multiply my problems?

'You were right as usual, Daddy,' she would tell the old man as soon as she was with him safe and sound. 'When you gave me those horses, you were right.'

'When that husband of yours has gone through all your competence,' old Robinette had said, in one of his rare telephone calls to her. 'Horses are a real comfort if you treat them right. You'll get a bit of income from them too, keep you going till you come to your senses and come back to me where you belong.'

There was no money in horses just now, but even so their presence cheered her.

The horses still went round and round as if they were controlled by an invisible ringmaster. A little of the old spirit rose up in Della; she would have liked to catch the horses, caress their elegant heads, she would have liked to ride horse-back in their perfect circle or ride far away over the hills as she had done years ago with Eugene at her side. Why should any Greek maiden fall in love with a bull when there were creatures like these around? It was a pity that she would be gone from here before the summer, she could have garlanded flowers about their necks. She stood quite still, like a child again, waiting for the swish of the ringmaster's silent whip.

The boy was waiting for her at the window. 'I've made some milky coffee. I've left it in the pan to keep it warm. I've got some dry clothes out for you and I've got an egg ready just like you said.'

Her clothes were soaking wet just as his had been.

'I'm not letting you go out in that cold any more. I'll take care of you. I'll fetch and carry and you won't know me from now on. I've made the fire and I'll get the coal.'

He had made bottled coffee. It was bitter, a kind she did not like. She warmed her hands around it and she sipped it for his sake.

'I'll work for nothing, Missus. You can have my wages.' She would get ready and go out again in a minute as soon as she had time to rest. She would find the penicillin, go out and dose the bull.

'Can I stay here for ever?' the boy asked her.

'For ever? How can I say?'

'For ever and ever?' the boy went on.

'I'm not sure what will happen to any of us once this snow goes.'

He got himself some water and she saw that his face was very white.

'I can stay here for a long time though, can't I?'

'We'll see, Daniel. We'll see.'

She stood up and buttoned her anorak again.

'I'll go out, Missus. Let me.'

'No. I'll have to give the bull an injection. It's coughing its lungs up like you said.' In the kitchen cabinet she sought out the medicine box.

'I can give injections, Missus.'

'No, I can't trust you to do that. Don't worry, I'm not going to run off and leave you, you know. Not yet. Where could I go in this snow?'

He looked at her sideways, but solemnly. 'All right, Missus. And when this snow goes, you'll stay here, won't you?'

'There's no telling that,' she said, speaking honestly. 'There's absolutely no way of knowing what the thaw might bring.'

The bull was very very ill; there was no denying it. She could

[116]

hear the cough quite plainly now this time as she neared its shed. Even the wind couldn't drown it out. She had brought along a syringe and an ampoule of penicillin which Rixon held illegally. She prepared to inject the bull. She was frightened but not for her own safety. This time she was afraid for the pain she would cause the bull. 'I'm not going to hurt you, not if I can help it,' she said. 'So just try to be brave, old girl.' Then she put in the needle and pressed the liquid in. There was silence and for a few seconds the coughing stopped as if the bull had drawn in its breath with surprise. She pulled back the syringe and stepped backwards, smiling at her success. But as she was leaving the shed the coughing started again. 'It will take a little time before it starts to work,' she explained and she wondered whether she should stay there and see the recovery process through or whether she should leave the shed and go back into the house. 'You'll be better in no time now,' she said and then as she was reopening the door she wondered why she had called the bull a girl.

It was necessary to alert Rixon to tell him that if the penicillin did not work his precious bull might die. In addition, the sheep which were under the mounds couldn't last much longer, unless you were prepared to believe the folklore about survival under the snow. If the bull died, there wouldn't be much point in having a farm. And, perhaps she ought to warn him, that in weather like this the boy might get up to one of his idiotic pranks and he might die. And then she could add that the way her energy was failing, *she* might die.

'So, you'd better line up one of your nice rich lady customers, Tom,' she would say to him, 'because, believe me, the way things are going, it's going to cost some money to put this place right.'

The thought of Rixon spending someone else's money made her feel more cheerful. The idea of this other woman sharing the old vicar's bed with him didn't trouble her and she looked forward to telling him so as she made her steep climb back into the house.

'Hugh phoned,' the boy said when he greeted her.

'Hugh?' The name seemed strange.

'Wanted that letter. The one the postman brought you never sent it. He wanted that book too.'

The letter waited on the mantelpiece.

'Played hell with me because I couldn't read. He said when he was teaching me at Christmas, I didn't try.'

'That's right, you didn't. As usual, you were fooling around. Is he phoning back?'

'I don't know. He didn't say.'

She sank back in a chair: 'That snowbank's getting steeper. I nearly didn't make it this time. And you were supposed to be at the window to help me in. What will happen if I slip and break my leg on the ice?' He had let the fire go down and she would have to make it up as soon as she had strength enough. She shivered from the cold.

The boy wandered upstairs, complaining, mumbling, asking how the hell he could be at the window. He'd been answering the phone to Poncy Hugh and he couldn't be everywhere at bloody once. 'I can never do anything right,' he said.

'That's the one thing we have in common,' Della said.

Rixon said: 'I'll never be able to afford another animal like that.'

She thought of Eugene's money and of the bull's hot feverish eyes.

'I'll get on to the Insurance Office, see what I can swing.'

'Swing?'

'Insurance I'm talking about, can't you hear?'

The bull had drawn in its breath in fear and agony as she inserted the needle. Thinking of this, she said: 'He isn't dead yet, you know.'

'What's that?'

'The penicillin might just hit the spot.' She no longer called the bull 'It.' She had begun to call it 'He', and now she always got the gender right. 'Anyway, I've done all I can. Why don't you contact a vet instead of an insurance man? But I doubt if they'll airlift a vet out on the National Health. I don't feel sure they'd airlift a doctor out to me or Daniel. We're forgotten people him and me.'

She heard an indrawing of Rixon's breath as if someone had just stuck a needle in him; he was shocked into silence like the bull. When he spoke again his voice indicated concern: 'Why are you talking like that? There isn't anything wrong with you, is there? If there is, say so. I'll get there somehow, a bit of snow won't stop me if you need me.'

'You mean you'd hijack a plane?'

'I mean I'd walk, dig my way in.'

'Strangely enough, one part of me still believes you would.'

'There isn't any question of it. If you're ill, I'll come.'

'Well, to let you off the hook, at the moment I'm as all right as any woman with a touch of arthritis and pains in the side and varicose veins could be after climbing out of a bedroom window and back again several times a day. Feeding animals, saving lives, digging sheep out of the drifting snow.'

'That's all right then,' Rixon said.

'I'm not complaining.'

'Sometimes, Della, you do your best to worry me.'

The telephone seemed to have become too heavy for her cold hands: 'I'd hate to do that. Under no circumstances could I bear to worry you.'

'I've changed my mind about staying here for ever,' the boy said.

She still shivered from the pain she had caused the bull and from the sight of the poor sheep buried in the snow. She now wondered if she had pierced the bull's vein at all or if she had a hit a muscle by mistake. Perhaps now, between its coughing spells, it moaned with pain, caused by her. 'I've cut my leg on something,' she told the boy. 'I'd better clean it up a bit.' She searched for iodine and cotton wool. 'Did you hear me telling Mr Rixon I'm very worried about the bull? I'll have to go out again in an hour or so.'

[119]

'I hate that old bull.'

'Well, I'm not crazy about it myself. But I don't like to see an animal in pain. It coughs and coughs and coughs.'

'Where I'm going to in America, there won't be any bulls,' the boy said. 'I've had enough of farms, they make me sick.'

She sighed. 'I wish I'd paid more attention to the vet when he came to inject the animals. I should have watched him closely. I could have learned exactly how it was done. Come to think of it, I could get some advice over the phone. He won't come here with all this ice and snow, but he might tell me what to do. Why didn't I think of that before?'

'It's like you said, Missus. I've been thinking. If I go and be a cowboy, I'll be stuck with cows. That's what you do if you're a cowboy; it's not all horses, stands to reason. When you were out, there was a man talking on the transistor. He went to America and he got a job in a big factory making cars. Then he met a lot of men and they protected people and they got very rich. Then *he* protected people and *he* got very rich and all these men did everything he told them to.'

'Very nice. I'd like to have a lot of men doing everything I want. But if I were you, I'd try to limit myself to borrowing car components from the factory. You could assemble them into cars at home at nights. It'd take you longer to get rich than it took that man you're telling me about, but you can be too ambitious. And then, if you do really well, those nice men you're talking about might come and offer to protect you.'

'I'll make cars all day and I'll protect people all night. Then I'll get to be a millionaire and I'll get a racing car: Zoom, zoom, zoom.' His hands manipulated the wheel.

'Right; but let's keep the driving till that day comes.'

'Zarroom, zarroom. You wait till I get to America. Just you wait, Missus. I'll show you then.'

'What I'd like is a little more concentration on here and now. We've got this storm to get through. And after that, you've still got a lot of your committal time left. I'm not sure that the Americans will rush to give you a visa. You've got a police record and, worse, you've got no money. I don't want you to go building up your hopes, you're always talking about going to America. You might be disappointed. Why don't you just try to do better for yourself here?'

'I don't like it here.'

'Well, there's no point in always living in the future. You're like Mr Rixon; he's been living in the future all the years I've known him. He's postponed his life until it's three-quarters over.'

Eugene had lived in the present, what little there was of it for him: 'No use even thinking about that, till I get home for good and all.' Eugene had said that several times and she remembered his nice, sad smile. A tune came into her head from the time when Eugene was alive. The Andrews Sisters; she could hear the tune, but what were the words? They had gone. But she recalled the theme: the sisters sang about the rights of women who stayed at home. She hummed it. How did it go? Too long ago to think back now. Eugene smiled his sad smile because MacArthur said that old soldiers never die. 'What he means is that they fade away.' But Eugene was wrong, they didn't fade away, they stayed with you over the years, coming out to haunt you when times were good and to be a comfort to you sometimes when times were bad like now. Maybe if your husband died of a slow illness, maybe if you actually saw him go, then you could believe it. But with Eugene it had happened too far away in a split second on a summer afternoon. They didn't fade away, they stayed with you, even after you had married another man, brought up that man's son.

'What will I have to do to get there?'

'You'll have to develop some skill, something the Americans want.'

'How can I do that?'

'You could try working hard. Try keeping out of trouble. Learn to read.'

'Yes, then I can write to you when I go. Hugh's getting me a special book from television. He's going to bring it next time he comes. So I'll be able to write to you every day once I've gone.'

'I can hardly wait,' Della said. 'But you're assuming I'll be here myself to read them.'

'I'll write to you wherever you are if I can write.'

They had sung 'Old Soldiers Never Die', when she had been a little child at school. But she was not sure that she understood the words even now. Maybe 'they only fade away' referred to what she had experienced in the years that had gone by since the shell exploded in Pusan. She tried to recall more of the song. Was it before or after Eugene was blown up that a kind of blanket began to cover part of her mind? 'What in hell's name does that matter?' she said aloud and then, aware that the boy did not know what she was talking about, she added: 'You and me, we'd better turn our minds to what's going on here and now. We've enough worries at this farm to keep us happy for the time being.' She thought back once more to Eugene. 'You can worry about the future at a later date.'

'I should have done this from the beginning,' she said, as she telephoned the vet. 'No, Mr Rixon should have done it, instead of worrying about insurance. It's *his* bull. Sometimes I find it hard to understand the workings of his mind.' The number had a double ring, it rang loudly and then she heard an echo of the sound the bell made, but there was no reply. She looked into the directory to see if there were other numbers she might ring, but her heart was sinking: 'There's no one there, Daniel. And even if I found another vet, they'd not come here, how could they? We'll have to manage on our own.' The boy was fiddling with the television set, he did not seem to be listening to what she said. 'In fact,' she complained to him, 'it's worse than being on my own. All you are is an added worry. I'll have to manage by myself.'

The bull was lying down now. It gasped for breath and she poured cough medicine down its throat, but this was a mistake: it caused the animal to cough and splutter more and she saw the medicine trickle back. But when she left, there was a momentary lull. Perhaps a little of the mixture had hit the spot. She should have tried this remedy earlier. The boy, to give him credit, had suggested this. She would dose it regularly and she allowed herself a little optimistic hope, that perhaps she had found the answer at last.

The boy was watching television when she got back, an educational programme about a settlement of Eskimos. The camera ranged over and over the snow. 'This is a nice change for us,' Della said. 'Perhaps they'll have a blizzard soon. We could do with some light entertainment for January viewing.'

'I can't get bloody ITV.'

'Well, try bloody BBC. Anything is better than this.'

The boy began to switch channels, he was going off in one of his angry states. Only the Eskimos came over clearly; the silent women and the laughing men. The only thing Della had ever really known about Eskimos was that they were said to lend their wives out to visitors: 'You may laugh together,' they were said to say. She wondered if Rixon would lend her out. Would he part with her for the price of a combine harvester or a pig? Probably so. Would he sell her, for example to old Robinette? YOU MAY LAUGH WITH MY WIFE STOP FOR THE PRICE OF A THOUSAND ACRE FARM. The credits came up on the screen and then the programme changed. A train wreckage somewhere; she thought of Hugh and worried. She looked at the smoking wreckage and she thought of all the places in the news: China? Rhodesia? Georgia? The train could have been going anywhere, the sound-track was too faint to tell. She tried to turn up the volume.

'Stop messing about with it,' the boy said.

'There's something wrong with the volume.'

The snow from the Eskimos film seemed to have remained within the set, white interrupted lines ran down the screen. The boy paced the room. The picture on the screen contracted into a small bright dot. Della watched the dot, then saw it fade. The boy stood near her and they watched the empty screen.

'You've broken it.'

She tapped the set and then took her hand away as if the screen were boiling hot.

'You never let me do the things I like.'

'Don't start that.' Had snow tampered with the roentgen rays? Could they become shattered, weakened, waterlogged, snowlogged? Could they die?

The boy slammed the set with his big powerful hand. He switched the knobs violently and then he thumped the set again. Then he wheedled at it: 'Come on. Come on.'

'It isn't any use. You'll have to say goodbye to Kojak till the thaw.'

The lower lip protruded.

'It isn't fair.'

'Nothing is fair.'

But inside her, she felt as the boy did. What would they do in here together without those nice screen faces to tell them jokes, to make them laugh, to sing them songs, to tell them what the weather would be like? How would the boy survive? What would she do with another link cut off? But she said: 'There's no point in moping. That won't get us anywhere. We've still got the transistors and the telephone and the light, thank God. And we've still got food and heat. Let's look on the bright side.' Count our blessings, sing a little hymn, peckers up, stiffen our lips. Look for the silver lining. 'Why don't you phone one of your friends and have a chat. Ask them what the snow's like in the village now. Find out what's going on? A trouble shared is a trouble halved or so they say.'

'What are you talking about? I haven't any bloody friends.'

And, come to think of it, has every cloud a silver lining?

'Those boys you hang about with at the billiard room.'

Was there a silver lining in Pusan?

'There must be one at least who has a telephone.' She looked at the boy through narrowed eyes. Was there a silver lining to the cloud the day his mother died?

Obeying the strictures of the BBC, she unplugged the set and

[124]

then sat for a time, still in her damp clothes, holding the plug helplessly in her hands.

Exhausted by the day, Della sought sleep. She sat back in her armchair, head back, feet crossed at the ankles. The cat stretched at her feet. The great fire she had made was warming to her, it influenced her dreams. In her dreams she and a boy who was alternately Hugh and alternately Daniel strolled in a pleasant snowless street. They stopped to look in the antique window of a shop. She touched a swirl in the glass with her finger, exploring it. Sometimes she half awakened to seek a more comfortable position.

In the chair, the other chair, the boy feigned sleep. His hands were folded under his chin like those of a child. She thought drowsily how they had just had a long conversation and that she had promised not to lose her temper with him any more. In return, he had promised to be better behaved and not to annoy her in future.

Once she woke up completely and looked anxiously at the grandfather clock. Then she remembered that this was another evening when Rixon would not be coming home. That makes one mouth less for me to feed she thought. And his mother will see to it that he's well taken care of; the table will be filled with all his favourite foods. She dozed again. The bull did not appear in her dreams at all. In her subconscious mind, she found herself planning a meal for herself and for the boy. Not the steak and burgundy, something else, something light. The boy loved beans. Should it be beans on toast? No problem there.

The dream had changed to some grassy bank, somewhere familiar, a place she had known long ago. Daisies and buttercups grew in abundance, grew so high that they were almost drowned in them, drowned in flowers. They rolled in the long, luxurious grass together. They? Even in the dream she was surprised by the plural. She drifted into a deeper sleep, slipping away from the snow, away from the farm and all its problems. They lay arms about each other, in buttercups and daisies and in tall, sweet grass.

'What have I done to deserve a girl like you?' he asked her. She felt his hands on her: 'Marvellous, marvellous, marvellous,' she heard his voice telling her. Yellow and white, yellow and white, the smell of the fresh grass. 'Marvellous, marvellous, marvellous girl.'

The boy stretched out his long, awkward legs. Then he curled up his nose to shake off a sudden itch. The Missus slept with her mouth open and she looked like an old sheep. He tapped his shin bone several times to the rhythm of one of the songs that went on in his head, deep inside himself. 'Don't tell the trees, 'cos the trees don't need to know.' He pursed his lips as if to whistle. 'An' dey will tell de birds and bees and everyone will know—' Silently, he rehearsed both parts and then he tapped his shins a little more loudly. He looked over at Della, giving her his sly look, even though she was asleep. She had told him that she was very tired, and he saw that her tights were torn and her legs were bruised. She had told him that she had had a very bad attack of that pain in her side and that she might not be able to carry on. He turned his head slightly to the side, but his eyes remained on her face: 'Rotten old witch,' he whispered.

'Marvellous, marvellous,' the voice in Della's dream insisted. 'Yellow and white, yellow and white.'

The boy decided that one day he would tell Della to go to hell. 'Go and take a running jump at yourself,' he would say. 'Ugly old bitch, that's what you are. Snoring like a pig.' He would buy himself a pure white suit, the kind of suit she said he could not buy and he would grow his hair to a length she would not permit and he would smoke Woodbines all day long. He would have one ear pierced and he would have a golden earring in it. He would get a silver pendant and a big white car and he would drive away from here.

'We could go a long, long way together, Della.' Rixon's body crushed her, his face was hot on hers and when he spoke he spoke in Eugene's voice. She stirred slightly in her sleep.

'Pig face,' the boy hissed at her. 'Pig-faced pig.' His spirit left the ugly, thick-walled house and drove away in Rixon's car, tore along snow covered highways at the speed of light, never swerving till he found a field somewhere, a field full of beautiful people, people with faces just like Hugh's, like Della's face had been when she was young. The boy stood up, tapped the side of his imaginary guitar, wakened the cat with a kick, then positioned himself, one foot forward, and drew in a long long breath.

'Marvellous, marvellous.' The scent of the flowers was strong. Della stirred. Her eyes opened and she looked at him and smiled. 'It's funny the things that come into your head when you're asleep,' she said.

'I'll put the kettle on,' the boy said. 'I expect you'll want a cup of tea.'

'Marvellous, marvellous,' Della said.

<hr />

In order to pass the rest of the afternoon amicably, she decided to give the boy a reading lesson.

'Then when you can read, you can move away from here. There aren't many jobs you can do if you can't read and write.'

'Have I got to move away then?'

'A few hours ago, you were all for it, weren't you? You always say you hate farms, especially this one. But I shouldn't worry. Neither you nor I will be moving anywhere just yet. It's snowing again. We might as well settle to something useful.'

'Well, all right then. But I haven't got that book that Hugh was going to get me. How can I learn without that, I'd like to know? Hugh says you can watch that programme and then read it all in a book. He says I'll soon learn that way because I like television.' He had his elbow crooked over his head, a pose he adopted when he wanted to avoid questions or work.

'Well, we haven't got the book and we haven't any television either, so we'll have to do with paper and with the books we have got.'

'It won't be any good without *that* book.'

'Don't be silly, you could learn to write by scratching in the snow with a stick if you put your mind to it.'

'Hugh said—'

'Hugh puts silly ideas into your head.'

He went over to the davenport, wanting to grumble about her plans, but not quite daring to. He brought a pad of paper and a thick lead pencil and she wrote out for him his name: 'Dan', the letters D.A.N. 'O.K., Copy that.'

He sat at her feet.

'Is that my name?' He bit at the pencil.

The telephone rang, interrupting him: 'I'll get it, Missus.'

'No you won't. You get on with that. I'll answer it.'

She picked up the telephone.

'No offence, but—'

'Oh, yes—' the boy looked up at her.

'It's his Uncle Charlie,' the voice said.

'Yes?—'

'I'm ringing about the lad,' Dan's Uncle Charlie said.

'Well?'

'I don't want any trouble—'

'But?'

'I've been in touch with his gentleman, the one who sees to him. I've been ringing him just to check up how the lad's going on.'

The social worker. Damn! Della thought, remembering that she had forgotten to phone to explain the missed appointment.

'Yes, I rang him to see how he was getting on.'

'Really. Did you? How exceptionally kind.' As Uncle Charlie spoke she could tell that he was chewing on his filthy pipe, the only filthy thing in Auntie Millie's house. He had been chewing on it the day he had brought Dan to the farm. A cheap pipe worn out by Uncle Charlie's ugly teeth. He had almost ground the stem away. His mouth sounded occupied.

'Like I say. I don't want to make any trouble, but it's the way you're treating that poor lad.'

Della was silent, she prodded the boy with her toe, directing him to write.

'Sounds to me like he's a prisoner.'

'A bird in a cage, you mean?'

There was a cough.

'Never gets out to see his pals.'

Then another sentence drowned out by the sucking on the pipe.

'No offence, but his auntie and me have always tried to keep an eye on him ever since my sister died. I mean it's the least we could do with her going young like she did and leaving him. We promised that we'd always see him right and we've always stuck to that.'

'Commendable,' Della said.

The boy was working hard, copying his name: 'D.A.N., D.A.N., D.A.N.,' he wrote. She thanked God that his poor dead mother (or was it his departed father?) had given him a name which would contract to those three simple letters. Though she, herself, always called him by his full name, three letters was enough for him to write.

'With us not having any of our own—' she tapped the telephone receiver with her finger. Uncle Charlie's voice filled the room. 'So, I'll put it this way. This is what I've got a right to know—'

The boy looked frightened, she prodded him again: 'N.A.D.,' he wrote. She pointed to the copy with her stockinged foot, correcting him: 'D.A.N., D.A.N.'

'The trouble is his auntie and me we don't feel that you're doing right.'

'A.N.D., A.N.D.'

'Well, well, Uncle Charlie. As a matter of fact, you may be right. Daniel is always saying that he's had enough of this farm. "This *bloody* farm", he calls it, if you want to be precise. Daniel is a boy who calls a spade a spade. He was, as a matter of fact,

[129]

just outlining his plans for his return to urban life. The word
"urban", Uncle Charlie, means "town". in case you didn't know.
T.O.W.N. Daniel has never been a country boy. No, the town
is definitely the place for him. I think his predilection may be
for a car factory and he might do better in Birmingham, but I
don't think he's quite ready to strike out on his own and as he
has such loving relatives in Manchester, I'm sure he can be diverted into some other industry. Posts and Telecommunications
might appeal to him. In any case, Birmingham is no use. I'd
forgotten. The social worker will remind you, the next time
you're having one of your little chats, that there's still a supervision order out on him and it was quite specific as I understand
it, he has to live with a willing family. And where you live
there'll be some nice conveyor belt you can get him on. Or,
better still, he could come in with you. There must be scope in
the plumbing trade. I've always been surprised how much goes
on in drains; much more than meets the eye. So, Uncle Charlie,
I'll tell you what to do, you come and get him now. Bring a
bulldozer though, he may need a little digging out.'

The boy looked up and she smiled down at his frightened,
crooked face. For the first time she noticed that he had cut his
hair, spikes of it stood up, defying gravity around his face. He
had been trying to please her.

'Daniel is *your* nephew, not mine.'

The boy stabbed at the paper with his thick pencil, he made
holes in the page and mouthed at her: 'No, no, no.'

There was silence at the other end of the line, even the
sucking on the pipe had stopped. Then there was a knocking as
if Uncle Charlie were emptying his pipe.

'And I do hope that when he's living with you, you'll do better
than we have. You'll be able to devote more time to him, you'll
be able to teach him to read, things like that. You'll be able to
guide him like a father, keep him far away from cars.'

There was another spate of knocking and then: 'You're
barking up the wrong tree, Missus. I wasn't suggesting anything like that. I'm only phoning just to get an idea if he's going

[130]

on all right. I'm just trying to put his Auntie Millie's mind at rest. She's been very poorly the last few months. It's her chest.'

'On top of her nerves?' Della said, clicking with her tongue. 'Well, your troubles are over. Daniel's very good with chests. He can give her a daily rub with camphorated oil. I'll let him practise on the bull.'

'Look, you've got me wrong, Missus. His auntie's very poorly, very very poorly. Can't do with any extra. I'm sure she couldn't take the lad on now.' There was agitation in the tapping sound.

'Well, Uncle Charlie, just before you ring off, I'll tell you this. If I have any more of these telephone calls from you or from his poor old aunt, if I hear so much as a wheezing on this line, I'll send him to you on the next dog sleigh out of here. So I'd advise you to think before you ring again.'

She reached down and she made herself touch the boy's mangled hair, gently, smoothing it in the right direction, as if he were the cat. 'Dan,' she said, 'it's D.A.N., not N.A.D.' It was the first time she had ever used the familiar version of his name.

His arm reached up again above his head and the light from the fire caught it and it looked for a second as if it were aflame: 'And don't go letting Uncle Charlie worry you.' The boy looked up at her with his twisted head, his eyes were for once focusing on her straight. 'He won't phone here again in a hurry, I can guarantee you that.'

The boy looked at her, managing his briefest smile.

'Come on now,' she said.

D.A.N. spells Dan.

❄❄❄

For ever afterwards, she told herself, I shall remember the sound of snow, the noise it makes. Even when the snow seemed still, there was a whistling in the silence. They must protect themselves, she told herself. She and the boy must secure their position, make sure there was enough to eat and drink. Make sure the animals would not starve. Make sure there were enough dry clothes, enough oil, enough coal. She must try to keep the boy's mind occupied, divert his thoughts from television. She would carry on with his reading lessons, conserve the battery in *her* transistor so that he could use *his* freely for his pop shows. Deprived of the chance to listen to the radio programmes she herself would have chosen, she had to accommodate to the ones he chose, she had to be content with his drums, his guitars, his screaming idols. There'll be enough time for symphonies and operas later, she reassured herself and she saw herself walking into the stalls at the Met on the old man's arm. She would wear some kind of white dress and she saw herself with flowers in her hair. But for now she decided that she must thank her lucky stars that she still had fire and light and access to the outside world and radio of a kind and still, by some miracle, telephone. This was no time to think of the icing on the cake. Why and how had the electricity and the light survived the gales, she wondered. The telephone was chancey up here at the best of times. She reported on the essentials of all the telephone calls to the boy in order to keep him in touch with the outside world: Rixon wanting daily roll calls, lists of the animals which had perished in the night. Hugh pestering her about his letters and his book. 'Neither of them gives a damn about me,' she said. Nor did they inquire about the boy, but she did not tell him this. And even the Western Union Man did not seem interested in any relevant aspect of her health. He ought to be asking if my ears have dropped off with frost or if I've been crushed by an avalanche. But, no, all I get are cables about my alimentary system or bulletins on old Robinette: CHEST IMPROVES LEAPS AND BOUNDS STOP, the last cable said. KEENLY AWAIT YOUR COMING STOP. She remembered that she had told the Western Union Man to cable him that she would soon be on her way. COMMUNICATION OF INTENT FILLS MY HEART WITH JOY STOP. They would see all the Broadway shows together. She had never seen the Grand Canyon; they could do that now. Though first she must catch up on the Caribbean sun. IS REMARK ABOUT

[132]

SUMMER DIARRHOEA INTENDED IN HUMOROUS VEIN STOP
MEANING OF THIS ELUDES ME STOP OR IS IT SOME SUBTLE
CODE. Summer Diarrhoea, she pondered. CABLE BACK IMME-
DIATELY IF SERIOUS MESSAGE INTENDED OTHERWISE SHALL
ASSUME JEST STOP AND IGNORE STOP BEG YOU AVOID FLIP-
PANCY IN DEALINGS WITH YOURS TRULY STOP YOU WILL
RECALL I AM A SIMPLE MAN.

'I didn't tell you to put that bit in the cable. You can just
cable back and explain it. At Western Union's expense.'

'I thought a little joke might do his chest good.'

'Not *his* chest. He never did like jokes. But never mind, I'll
send another cable now. Tell him I'll be with him as soon as I
can after the snow goes. Wild horses won't keep me here once
there's a sign of the mercury going up.'

She made a call to the boy's social worker.

'Still snowed in?' the social worker said. 'Dear me, the police
will be wondering what to do with their time.'

Della made a sound with her mouth, loudly enough to make
the social worker think again. 'Just a little joke, Mrs Rixon.
There's nothing really wrong with Dan. No, he has a great
deal of potential. He's a little too easily led that's all.'

'He's perfectly all right when he's with me,' Della said. 'I
never have any trouble with him. It's all in the way you handle
him.'

The social worker said nothing for a time and then he said:
'Well, I'll be seeing him next week, as usual, will I?'

'Of course, always supposing that we're out of here. It could
be that the house might collapse and smother us. That would
ensure an endless holiday for the police. It's an ill wind, they
say.'

'Mrs Rixon, you do say some funny things.'

'I'm laughing off my troubles,' Della said.

'Well, I don't suppose getting out of there will present much
of a problem really; not for a nifty lad like Dan.'

To compensate for the television going off, she searched out all the old photographs to show the boy. Seaside scenes when Hugh was small, a trip to Boulogne with Eugene, Rixon and her cruising up the Rhine. She held out a picture of Hugh. 'That's Hugh,' she said. 'He used to have such a serious face. He laughs more now.' Was he no longer serious? Or did he only laugh to disguise the fact that he had nothing to say to her and his father? She shrugged off the thought. A picture of Della next. Della hitch-hiking in the Lake District, a rucksack on her back, a bright smile on her face, trouser leg rolled up. Della, inviting attention, grinning, thumb jerking, as if to attract a passing car. 'My mother never liked me to go hitch-hiking, but nothing ever frightened me in those days.'

'Did your mother think you might get murdered?'

Della's hair was blonde on that picture, sunbleached, streaked.

'Murdered? Good Heavens, no.' She searched for a word. 'Attacked. I expect she thought I might get attacked.'

'Maybe she thought you might get raped.' The boy held the snapshots delicately, making sure that he did not get his fingers on the shiny parts.

'Attacked, I said.'

His eyes narrowed as he looked at a picture of Della in a gymslip with her friends. She was the tallest, blondest girl. She took the picture from him.

'Did anybody?'

'What?'

'Attack you?'

'Of course not. Though I daresay I had one or two narrow escapes.' She sorted through the snapshots.

'What did your mother say?'

'I don't suppose I told my mother.'

'Why?'

'Children don't tell their mothers everything.' Take Hugh, for example, take him and his Bloody Bee. 'Sometimes your mother is the last person you'd tell.' In any case, did anyone ever tell you any of the things that mattered? Did Rixon? Had Eugene? Had he told her about that mission? 'I'm nothing but a cypher clerk,' he'd said. 'No danger there.'

She looked at the picture of herself in her gymslip. Her hair pulled back tidily so that her pretty child's face was visible. Her body was no longer a child's body on that picture, it had begun to cause problems. The gymslip no longer fitted it. She stood with her arms folded and she rounded her shoulders to compensate. She cried a lot at that time too. She cried for her big feet, long legs and yellow hair. She cried because she was too tall, too fat. Her mother said she never cried when there were any men around.

'I used to be terribly sad in those days, Dan,' she said.

'Why were you sad, Missus?'

'I suppose I thought I'd never get what I wanted. A handsome husband, riches, diamonds, fame.'

'Did you?'

'I got the handsome husband.' Multiplied by two. 'That's Tom; Mr Rixon. Can't you see? That was one of the first times I ever went out with him. That one's of me. He took it of me standing near a cow. He said it was a waste of film using it on people. He always preferred an Ayrshire or a pig.' She watched the reaction on the boy's face. 'I was quite frightened of that cow. You'd never have thought I'd be pouring medicine into a bull, not if you'd known me then.'

The boy looked at the picture. 'Why did you marry old Rixon, Missus?'

'I must have wanted to.' She paused. 'Look, here's the first picture ever of me. Before all my cares began.'

The boy scratched a mark off Della's baby face. 'You've got no clothes on, Missus.'

'I was only a baby. It was the fashion then.'

[135]

'My mother wouldn't let anyone take mucky pictures of me.'

She put the picture to one side and searched the pile for a particular one of Hugh: 'Here, this is a nice one, though it's a little blurred. I think his father must have jerked the camera.'

The boy took it. 'Why doesn't old Rixon like Hugh?'

'Why do you say that?'

'He doesn't like him, you can tell.'

'There are times when you say very silly things, Daniel.' She had, she noticed, gone back to the full form of his name. 'All families quarrel now and then, it's natural.'

There were more pictures of Della. In some she was courted by the vicar's son, she saw herself pull away from his restraining hand. Then she was pictured receiving a prize from old Sir Edmond from the Manor House, an old man with fond hands and faded eyes, not quite willing to let go of the leather-bound copy of *Ivanhoe*, reluctant to release it into Della's young hands.

'I didn't ever read the odious thing. Filthy old pig,' she'd said.

'Why did he give you that book?'

'Because I was top of my form. You didn't know that I had brains.' The book was in this house somewhere with the pages still uncut.

'Missus, did that old Eugene have brains?'

'More brains than anyone else I ever knew. He always had his nose in a book. Not like me, I never read much. In some ways I was more like you.'

'Like me, Missus. You like me?'

She let a snapshot of her wedding to Rixon flutter to the ground. The boy picked it up and turned it sideways and she corrected its position in his hands.

'You know who that is, don't you?'

The boy looked away from the picture and he gazed around the room, at the dark opaque windows, at the bright chrome kettle, the blue and white tiles, the matching cretonne curtains and the sodden blankets which plugged the outer door.

'Don't pretend you don't recognize us. You know perfectly well who it is.'

Handsome, black-haired Rixon and herself, a beauty in her day. 'No bloody Yank is going to steal you from me, not this time,' Rixon said. Della smiled at the camera, to prove that she was not unhappy to end her widowhood. Nicely dressed in clothes a young girl now might have been quite glad to wear. Her prize-winning legs were almost covered by her New Look dress, a lacy hat covered her curly hair. Prize-winning bride: a lot of women would have liked to be in her shoes that day. But then a lot of men had wanted her: trim little widow, neat hands, neat feet, tidy little dowry in the bank.

'Dan, why don't you look? It's me and Mr Rixon on our wedding day.'

Had they changed that much?

'You and old Rixon on your wedding day?'

Eugene said she looked like Nancy Olson. Rixon said she was a Marilyn Monroe.

'Well.'

The sly smile and the big hand obscuring it.

'What are you grinning at?'

'You and old Rixon.'

She screwed up her eyes, trying to see the element of ridiculousness which had amused the boy. Rixon's hair? His suit? Her hat? Had she deluded herself about their good looks? Had she deluded herself about everything all her life?

She handed over a final picture of Hugh.

'Hugh punting under the Bridge of Sighs.'

'Size?'

'Sighs.'

She kept her hand on it.

'That's Hugh's closest friend. The one he was talking about. Remember he told you his father is a lord.' The thin hand of the lord's son trailed the water. 'Hugh went to stay at their place once, just before you came. I don't suppose he'll ever bring him here though.' Hugh was laughing at something the lord's son was saying, though from the look of him the lord's son was too tired to speak. He lay back on a cushion like an invalid.

'I always wanted Hugh to go to Cambridge. Mr Rixon says it's silly nowadays. But, even so, I put my foot down. I insisted some money was put aside to make sure Hugh got a chance.' Just like Eugene. She looked at the sunlight in the photograph. 'You can go and spend a day or two there sometime. Hugh could show you round. Maybe I can take you there; though maybe I shan't be here to do that. I'll pay your fare, you can travel on your own.' Hugh and the lord's son made a lovely pair. 'You'd have your work cut out to say which of them was fathered by a lord.'

'My Auntie Millie says your Hugh doesn't look like his dad.'

'Your Auntie Millie! How absurd.'

'She says he's like that old Eugene.'

'Your Auntie Millie should keep her silly thoughts to herself. She has no idea what Eugene looked like. He died three years before Hugh was born. She is a gossiping old bitch.'

When she first met Eugene he took her punting on the river too. 'Don't marry that English man,' he said. 'I mean it, Della. Give him his diamond back and come to the States with me.' She could see his face now in the punt, she could see it close to the face of the son of the Labour peer.

The boy took the picture from her hand and breathed on it and polished it with his hand. 'Your Hugh and that thin lad, Missus. Looks like they're a couple of poofters to me.'

❖❖❖

The Western Union Man had a headache and said he felt as if he were in need of one of the old man's remedies himself.

'I'm not feeling so hot either,' Della said. 'Thank God for the old man and his cables. He's a lifeline. Things are getting desperate here.'

'Tell me what kind of a lifeline you feel you need.'

'The first essential is a cure for bovine croup. That's my main problem now.'

She heard him shuffling the cables: 'Bovine croup. No, there's nothing about that, I'm afraid. And the old man is in the same boat as you and me and the bull. Not well. They're injecting him several times a day. Do you want the exact dosage they're administering? I've got it here. But he's beginning to lose all faith in modern medicine. He's into nature cures: HONEY AND SENNA PODS CURES EVERYTHING STOP. I wish I had some for my head.'

'You're feeling really ill?'

'Not good at all. My wife says I need a day in bed.'

'Sounds like a sensible woman.' So he was a married man; a man with a wife, a mortgage, a semi and a small garden to keep. But why should she feel disappointed? What was the Western Union Man to her? A voice? A laugh? An interruption in her lonely life? 'Why don't you do as the lady says?'

'What about the cables?'

'Let them take care of themselves for a day.'

'Who'll keep you up to date on the state of the Union if I do?'

'My cables will keep. Anyway, what about the other man?'

'Lumbago: he's already given in.' He sighed. 'These cables, they're not things you can ignore.'

'Nonsense.'

'You underestimate them, Mrs Rixon. Honey and senna pod, for instance, it might save the world.'

'What happened to gamma globulin, I wonder?'

'Too hard on the ageing gluteus, I should think. Honey and senna pods goes in by mouth.'

'He's open-minded, I'll say that for him. For a man of his age, he's always ready to try anything new.' She heard the crackling of paper again. The ticker tape? She decided that she must ask him about the mechanical process by which the messages were received. Why in all her years of getting cables had she never wondered that before? The crackling stopped.

'Back to work,' the man said. 'Are you listening? MAXIMUM DOSAGE CONSTITUTES SURE-FIRE CURE.'

'Sure-fire cure for what?'

'INTERNAL AND EXTERNAL ILLS.'

'Name some.'

'Measles, rubella, Asian flu.'

'No good. I haven't any of those.'

'Bronchitis, typhoid, ulceration, hepatitis, abrasions, this and that.'

'Would honey and senna pods help this bull?'

The Western Union Man seemed to laugh, a short, sharp laugh which might have been a cough: 'Look I told you I couldn't abandon my post, the rest of these cables are in a different vein. He hardly dwells on medicines at all. I couldn't leave messages like this, not to the other man.' He cleared his throat: 'HAVE NEVER TRULY EXPLAINED EXTENT OF MY REGARD STOP FROM SICK BED NOW COMPELLED TO TELL YOU ALL.'

'You're making it up,' Della accused the man.

'I'm not: AFFECTION FOR YOU LIMITLESS STOP DEEP LOVE FOR YOU KNOWS NO BOUNDS MIND NEVER FREE OF YOU SINCE YOU LEFT DESERTING ME FOR PRESENT SPOUSE.'

'It can't be true.'

'You're not giving me time to put in the stops: GAPING HOLE LEFT BY SON CAN BE FILLED BY NOBODY BUT YOU. Then there's a stop.'

'Yes, stop,' Della said. 'Stop, stop, stop. You're embarrassing me talking to me this way.'

'SHALL NEVER REST,' the Western Union Man went on, 'TILL I SEE YOUR LOVELY FACE AGAIN. Lovely face? The old man is gone on you.'

'Yes, may God in his mercy give me grace. The old man has never used poetry before.'

'He's using it now. Sounds to me as if he's ready to give you the earth. There'll be no shortage of honey and senna pods for you from now on.'

She picked up a small hand mirror from near the telephone and looked at her face in it: 'My God, the poor old man *is* in for a shock. There's nothing lovely about my face now.'

'I don't believe a word of it—'

'Come clean. You did make it all up, didn't you? The old man never spoke to anyone like that.'

'God's honour. I'll send the cables on, you can read them for yourself.'

'I shan't get them. It's worse than ever here. I shan't be able to read them unless you get a spade and dig them in.'

'I'd dig *you* out with my bare hands if I had the strength. Believe me, I would.'

'I do believe you about that.'

'If it weren't for this terrible throbbing in my head.'

'Better try the old man's cure,' she advised him. 'Are there any more declarations from him to me today? Or has your inventiveness run out?

'WHEN I THINK THAT THE MOST BEAUTIFUL GIRL I EVER ENCOUNTERED WILL SOON TAKE HER PLACE AT MY SIDE—'

Her head swam. 'That's enough, I know he'd never say that. You're going too far.'

The Western Union Man did laugh a little now and then he said: 'No, I promise you, I wouldn't deceive you like that.'

'You're trying to boost my ego.'

There was a silence and then the man said: 'No, you underestimate yourself. You're something special.'

'Are those your words?'

'They're *his* words: "special", Della, I swear.'

But then there was a severe crackling on the line, louder than the sound of his voice, louder than the crackling of the paper. It was getting hard to hear what the man was saying. Perhaps he was trying to make her feel better, trying to reassure her, build her up.

'Have you ever wondered—' she started to say, wondering if he had ever wondered why the old man communicated by cable and not by telephone. But there was silence. She shook the receiver, but there was no sound at all.

The boy followed her into the passage.

'You and me, Dan.'

'Me and you?'

Snow had got in on the coal.

'So, it's up to us,' she said.

She picked off the top layer of coal with her hands and then she placed sacks over the rest. Now all we've got to do is to cut off the electricity, pour out the paraffin, run out of food, break an arm or leg. 'At least,' she told the boy, 'we're not likely to catch any diseases. We're safe from germs. Unless of course, there are any bacteria nesting in the snow, like those germs from the Antarctic they found in the ice a year or so ago.' She put the idea of catching an infection from the bull out of her mind, no point in mentioning that to him. 'And, you know what, with our luck, yours and mine, I wouldn't be surprised if a colony of microbes was taking over your snowman now.'

'Could a colony of microbes—?' the boy asked, picking up her fears.

She climbed out again to see to the bull; it was still coughing and a thin stream of blood had congealed on its jaw. It was lying down now. Della went up to the animal, very close to it, soothing it. Then she gathered up all her courage and injected it in its right flank: 'Gluteus maximus,' she whispered to it, speaking the name as tenderly as if she really were Europa, whispering endearments to the bull.

But this bull shook with pain: 'I'm sorry,' she said in English. 'Believe me, I wouldn't hurt you, I wouldn't cause you any pain, not if there was any other way.'

'Why don't children tell their mothers everything?' the boy nagged at her.

Her mind was on the bull: I should, she thought, have insisted on a vet flying in. What the hell is Air Sea Rescue for?

'Everything about what?' she asked.

'Everything about what they do. Like about you getting attacked by all those men.'

[142]

'I didn't say I got attacked. I said that my mother used to worry in case I got attacked.'

She purled a stitch she should have knitted. When the snow went he would spread the word around the village and the town that Della the bank manager's wife had wandered up and down the old highways jumping into cabs, easy prey for long distance lorry drivers. But why worry about that? There were many other things to worry about. In the United States the snow was more severe than this; what if some of their weather travelled over here?

'Does Hugh tell you everything?'

Hugh was a long way off.

'I don't suppose so. I've told you once, children keep things to themselves. They grow away from their parents. They're like birds, as soon as they can they leave the nest and set up on their own.' She was knitting a pair of socks for Rixon. She picked up stitches now turning the heel. Twenty stitches were required; she concentrated on counting them. Grey wool, soft, the kind he said he liked to keep him warm in winter.

'Why do they keep things to themselves?'

She could finish off this sock tonight, she could easily get to the toe if the boy would let her have some peace. Then she thought that if she could involve him, get him to wind some wool for example, he might keep quiet. He could put the wool over the back of the chair to stretch it whilst he wound it. It would give him something to do. Perhaps if they worked together they might avoid conflict during the snow. The boy would wind and she would knit; and together they would create a permanent supply of socks for Farmer Rixon's feet. It would be better if neither of them were idle; idleness left too much time for thought.

'Why do they keep things to themselves?'

'Children begin to want to keep their own counsel. They want privacy. First they start confiding in their friends and then they start confiding in their wives and husbands.'

But most of the thoughts which whirled around in her head these days could never be shared with Rixon. Could she tell him,

[143]

for example, that she spent a great deal of every day thinking about Eugene, that she spent hours talking to his ghost? Could she tell him that she pretended that she was still Eugene's wife and that she was happy to have the vicar's bed all to herself so that she could imagine that she shared it with Eugene? Could she tell Rixon of the plans for her escape from him? Was there anything important she could ever talk to him about? 'Children,' she said. 'They tell their mothers everything when they're little. Hugh was always running in with stories about things he'd seen or done. He used to tell me everything anyone said to him. But then he began to grow away from me: from us, I mean. All children do that.' She began to join up a new ball of wool, frowning because she had not foreseen that the join would come in an awkward place. That was what came of not having your mind on what you were doing, of not seeing what was coming up. She twisted in the threads of wool, hoping to avoid a knot which might be uncomfortable for Rixon's feet.

'But why don't they tell you anything?'

'Be quiet, Dan. You're making me make mistakes.'

'Just tell me then.'

She counted up to ten stitches in order to prepare a patient answer. It might even be possible to change the subject, to distract him from the repetition of this question. But nothing new came from her tired mind. Her needles clicked and then she said: 'You know, Mr Rixon doesn't like me knitting.'

'Why not?'

'The noise annoys him.'

'The noise of knitting?'

He cocked an ear listening to her needles.

'It gets on his nerves. But I tell him if he wants hand-knitted socks he'll have to put up with the noise. It's not as bad as his tractor, is it? It's not as noisy as his cows. I've always liked to have something useful to do. Even when I was married to my first husband and we had servants to do everything for us, I still used to find something to do; sewing, embroidery, painting, anything.'

The boy was silent, thinking over what she had said, his eyes fixed on the grey wool as it passed rapidly over her fingers. At last, she congratulated herself, he had forgotten his original question. She knitted three needles of stitches smoothly, pressing out the thickness at the join that she had made. Now that she had definitely decided to leave Rixon as soon as the snow had gone, she felt it was her duty to leave him well supplied with socks. He already had diverted most of her money to his own purposes, so there was little else that she could leave him. She knitted on, thanking God that the boy was silent, so that she was free to pursue her thoughts. As soon as the telephone was on again she must telephone old Robinette so that they could finalize her plans.

She would need bathing suits, beach dresses, evening dresses too. Yes, there would be many things to prepare before she left. The boy broke into her thoughts again: 'My mother could knit.' She was a little startled because he mentioned his mother rarely and because she had been told by his Uncle Charlie that he did not remember her at all. 'My mother could knit socks, pullovers, trousers, hats and coats.'

Shoes, Della's mind added, cars, tractors, jumbo jets.

He waved his big hands in the air, describing all the garments which had been created by his mother's knitting needles. 'My mother knitted better socks than them.'

'Did she?' she said aloud. 'That's nice. But I thought you had never seen your mother.'

'Never seen my mother?'

'After you were a baby, I mean.'

He hesitated, bit at his lip and then he clasped his hands around his knees: 'What are you talking about, Missus? She used to knit and knit and knit. She said it was best to keep your hands busy; she knitted all day long.' He rocked backwards and forwards, backwards, forwards, forwards, back. 'She knitted ten times better than you.'

'I daresay.' This pair of socks would soon be ready for Rixon, he could claim them from her as soon as the thaw set in. And

[145]

they might be the last pair of socks that she would ever knit. A pair of socks knitted silently so far as he was concerned. No needles to annoy him, just the finished product, a pair of grey socks knitted in the snow. She knitted on.

'I used to tell my mother everything,' the boy said. 'I wasn't like you and your bloody Hugh. I used to tell her everything I did.'

'Everything?' Her knitting became more rapid; knit, purl, knit, purl, knit. Another knit another purl.

'And if my mother was alive now, Missus, I'd tell her all about this snow. I'd tell her about that door when it wouldn't close and you sticking them blankets in. I'd tell her about them woolly bastards getting buried and I'd tell her about my snowman. And the way you made me go out in that bitter cold. And I'd tell her about you sticking needles into that poor bull. And you always talking to that Western Union Man and you laughing like you do. And I'd tell her about you running off with that old Robinette and leaving Mr Rixon on his own. And you telling my Uncle Charlie off and them rotten socks you're knitting and them needles: click, click, click. And about you making me stay in that bedroom with the ceiling coming in.' He was rocking back and forwards like someone in a trance. She faltered, another purl instead of a knit and she took the stitch back slowly.

'And I'd tell her you won't even let me go out. You're keeping me in prison here.'

Where was Hugh now? And what was going on in his secret, privileged life? What was he doing whilst she was penned in here with this irritating rocking boy? This boy was nothing to her, none of her blood and she felt a little anger for his mother who had opted out and left the boy to her. Why was she here, listening to him and his nonsense and simultaneously manufacturing socks for Rixon's feet? The needles stuck.

'Dan,' she said. Her voice was loud. He stopped rocking, frightened by her tone. He stared at her with his two uneven eyes and she started back as if she had never looked at him

[146]

before. Uneven eyes, uneven shoulders and ugly uneven hands. What did his mother think when they showed him to her? Poor woman. He would have been red, wizened, crooked and unformed. The sight of him must have driven the poor woman half into her grave, because whatever lies he told, the poor woman had died three days after he was born. He was born feet first, his Uncle Charlie said, head last, the wrong way up.

'I'd tell her you don't let me wear my own things either. You keep making me get dressed up in other people's clothes. What's wrong with my cowboy boots? I don't want to wear old Rixon's nasty wellingtons and coats. And I'd tell her that you don't care about me. You're going to America and leaving me. You don't give a damn what's going to happen to me.'

In spite of him the knitting had progressed.

'You care more about them smelly socks than you care about me.'

'That's enough,' she said at last. But she was not sure whether 'enough' meant that she had knitted enough rows on the instep and that now she had reached the straight. She knitted on rapidly, her blood racing because of the boy's words.

The bull's head drooped. She bathed its mouth to give it ease. Its hot frightened eyes fixed on her and made her frightened too.

'I think we're going to die,' she told herself. 'I wonder if any of us is strong enough to escape this snow.' She stroked the bull and smiled: 'That's nonsense, Pride. It isn't as bad as all that. I'm letting myself get fanciful. No one in this country ever perishes in snow.'

She looked sadly at the bull, wishing that there was a solution. Some medicine to stop the cough. Then she turned to go, wondering if she had the energy to climb back into the house.

The lights had begun to flicker and the boy had one of his frightened spells. Della had already sorted out all the candles she could find.

'I wish I hadn't had that old lamp connected up for electricity. I could have used it as an oil lamp now.'

'No one could get us, could they?'

'Get us?'

'Murderers? Could a murderer come and get us here?'

There was definitely something wrong with the electric lights; the power points were still working but the central light went on and off. She placed two candlesticks at the ends of the mantelpiece; she would allow only two candles at a time, more would be an extravagance, a danger to their light supply. They must rely on the light from the fire so far as they could. She wished that there was some way of getting the television going. It would occupy the boy's mind, put an end to all his questions and complaints. But at the same time, she was glad that he was not a reader. How would an avid reader like Hugh survive in this flickering light?

'You are funny, Dan. I really don't understand you at all. You go out in broad daylight and steal cars to go joy-riding in. You drive hell for leather along the motorway even though you've never had a lesson in your life. The magistrate said it was a miracle you'd not been killed. He said it was obvious you had no sense of fear. And yet you've decided you're afraid of being murdered now.'

'I'm not afraid. I'm not afraid of anything. I just don't want to be murdered, that's all.'

'Well, unless you drive *me* into murdering you, I'd say you were pretty safe here.'

The centre light flickered and went out. Della lit both the candles with a match.

'I saw something on television, Missus. An old woman and a boy. And they was at a farm.'

She waited, watching the small lamp on the top of the dead television set. She was reluctant to stop looking at it even though there was another source of light.

'Every light at that farm went out and then a man climbed in through the window to get that woman and that boy.' As he

[148]

spoke the last light did go out. Both of them looked at the curtain at the foot of the stairs.

'Climbed in through the bedroom window, did he? And did he have a dagger in his mouth?' She moved the candles and looked over her shoulders again, back at the slight movement of the curtains.

'Yes, Missus, he did. He had a dagger and a gun.'

'I call that being well prepared, I'd like to meet a man like that. You could rely on him in an emergency.' The boy was thorough in his lies, you had to grant him that. The cat appeared from nowhere, rubbing against her legs. 'Well, no one could get you here, so you can just stop worrying about that. I'll tell you this, if there were any chance of anyone getting to this farm, that person would be Mr Rixon. He's so crazy about this place, he wouldn't desert it like he has if it were humanly possible to get here. Not that he's likely to worry his head about you and me, but this place is his pride and joy and then he'll be very worried about the bull and the sheep and the money he might lose if they all die.'

'Missus, there might be a man here already, hiding in the buildings.'

'Fiddlesticks,' she said, watching the flickering candle-flame. 'Why should anyone want us dead?'

'Them Thompsons were dead, weren't they?'

'They weren't murdered.'

'No, but they were dead. The postman and them Varleys dug their bodies out.'

'Yes, but they weren't murdered, I keep telling you.' She pulled her cardigan around her. 'I think you enjoy feeling frightened. Why don't you think about something else?'

'Because there might really be a man.'

'Long John Silver with a parrot on his shoulder? Wearing half your pair of wellingtons and a dagger in his sock and a blunderbuss in his hand. Listen, I can hear him shouting "Pieces of eight". I can hear him stabbing into the snowbank with his wooden leg.' Pointed, strong, unable to feel the cold.

I almost wish I had one myself. I'd be free from chilblains, bruises, varicose veins. No need for honey and senna pods, not if you had a wooden leg. 'He'll be waiting in the bull's shed, waiting to steal our treasure. He'll be brushing icicles off his parrot at this very moment. Or maybe he's blowtorching the ice with his blunderbuss, melting it to make a path.'

The light touched the boy's face. He had picked up the cat and he was stroking it and for once it tolerated his touch.

'I saw a picture, Missus, really. This man was hiding in the shed and then he came out and cut that old woman's throat. Then he told the boy to shut up and the boy didn't and so the man shot him.'

'I don't blame him.'

'Then the boy crawled out—'

'Have you thought of a pack of wolves?' she asked him. 'There must have been pictures about wolves on television. A pack of them coming down from Scotland, drawn by the snow, attracted by the scent of the cattle.' By the lifeblood of the poor bull. She thought back to mythology; if you were dealing with myths why stick at murderers? 'Why not a killer shark swimming in the moat?'

'There isn't a moat.'

'That's no deterrent to a real story teller.'

'Will a murderer come?'

She looked straight at his candle-shadowed face.

'Why should anyone want to come and murder you and me? Unless you murder me and I murder you, we're perfectly safe. From murder anyhow.' Had he smelt death in the house? Was that why he asked her all these questions? Had it followed her in from the bull's shed? 'We're not going to get killed,' she said. But she herself was not quite sure about that, not with that snow falling, not with that layer of it on the coal, not with that fierce wind still blowing, not cut off, as they were, from telephones and electricity, not with that ancient tumbling roof.

'A burglar might come.'

'A burglar. Now you really are being fanciful.' She looked

[150]

around the room. 'What in hell's name would a self-respecting burglar bother to take away from here?'

The boy looked around the room too and then back at her as if her question puzzled him greatly. 'What about all this furniture?' he said. 'And that pair of candlesticks. Hugh said they're made of gold. And what about them lamps and ashtrays?'

'Dan, you shouldn't listen to everything Hugh says. Those candlesticks are brass. All the money has gone on animals and implements, there's nothing of any value inside the house. So stop worrying about burglars, you can rest assured, no one in his right mind would dig his way through all this snow to steal these bits and pieces. In fact, I doubt if you'd get a scrap dealer to take them away unless you paid him.'

The candlelight illuminated the brass candlesticks. 'What about your fur coat then?'

'No one is coming seven miles in a blizzard to steal that. Except maybe a another rabbit, or perhaps a cat.'

The boy let the cat jump from his knee.

'Your rings then?'

'Do you think anyone would saw my fingers off for a pair of rings like that?' It was hard to see the diamond at all in candle-light, the diamond with which Rixon had plighted his troth. 'This diamond,' she said 'is the smallest diamond in the world.' And yet, as always when she said such things, remorse and sadness filled her. Rixon's face came into her mind and she remembered that life had always been hard for him and that no one had ever left him money. 'You see, Dan, when Mr Rixon gave me this ring, he had very little money. To begin with he'd already given me one ring and we decided that that ring wouldn't do any longer and so he had to buy another. His family are quite poor and he's always had to help them. And he was only in the army then and he had to go without cigarettes for weeks to save up to get that ring for me. 'I'll get a better one,' he'd said. 'Just as soon as we get on our feet.' She had had to discard her wedding ring to put Rixon's little diamond on her finger.

'I remember it was a really nice day. We were in London and

we went for a walk along by the river and looked at the boats. And I kept looking at that little diamond.' And I kept looking at the gap on my finger where Eugene's gold band had been.

'A burglar might come and get your other rings. My Auntie Millie said you must have some lovely rings put away.'

'Would your Auntie Millie like a guided tour of this place sometime? She'd no doubt be disappointed when she saw that I haven't any beefeaters but she might like the narrow winding stairs and I daresay I could manage to produce a raven or two.'

She looked at the little ring on her finger and polished up the gold. 'What do your Uncle Charlie and Auntie Millie find to talk about when they're not talking about me? But you can tell your Auntie Millie she's quite right. I have them in a chest at the bank, a strong-box isn't big enough. And the only reason I don't wear them is that there are too many for my fingers and I never was any good at making decisions.'

No, she had told Eugene, I'm not interested in diamonds, not at all. A plain gold band is what I want this time.

'I told Mr Rixon: "This is the only fancy ring I'll ever wear. Just put my wedding ring next to it then I'll have all I want." So you can stop worrying about burglars, you can rest happily in your little bed. Honey and senna pods is all the riches *I've* ever been showered with.'

The jammed door moved inwards and they both turned towards it.

'A change in the weather,' she said. 'I'm sure I hear a wind getting up in the West now.' So, if the boy wanted to conjure up another film, what about one in which a forty-eight-year-old woman who'd been a beauty in her day smothered to death in the snow? Accompanied only by a sixteen-year-old boy. She put more coal on the fire and then she placed the usual shovel on the hob to draw it up. She reached for her knitting, telling herself that she was glad that at least there was one thing she could do well in the dark.

The announcer on the boy's transistor said that the Royal Air Force had airlifted a farmer and his family out from a hill farm in Northumberland. They had been picked up in a helicopter from somewhere quite near Hadrian's Wall. The boy turned off the transistor violently and said that he bloody well wished they'd airlift him out because he was bloody well fed up. And if Della wanted to know what he was fed up of, he was fed up of her and this rotten house and that rotten cat and her bloody needles clicking and the snow and of being bloody bossed about. He had got at Rixon's store of beer and his speech was slurred.

Della said that if a helicopter did come, she'd be aboard so quickly, he wouldn't be able to see her for dust. And that once she got on to that helicopter, that would be the end of her and that if she never saw Rixon and this place and him again it would be a damn sight too soon. And that if he touched Mr Rixon's beer again, she'd sling him out into the snow.

The boy said that he'd be bloody first on the helicopter, not her. And he would tell the helicopter man not to pick up that old witch. In any case, he could fly the helicopter himself. He'd been on one already. He'd flown it himself to give the pilot a rest. He'd flown all over Manchester and she needn't think he hadn't because he had. He gave her his sideways look and she knew that he was lying, of course, but she didn't know quite how much he was lying, because he might have flown in a helicopter at some time: orphanage children were often taken on the sort of sprees that never came the way of other children.

And then he said that when the helicopter did come, he'd get old Rixon's twelve bore and then if the pilot wanted to let her get on, he'd hijack the helicopter and if the pilot disobeyed his orders he would shoot him and her too.

She sighed.

It came back to her that she herself had once travelled in a helicopter. She had flown from Washington to La Guardia. The boy rushed about the room, making swishing noises as if he were an aircraft of some kind. She remembered that the flight of the helicopter had been smooth and static, there had been no sensation, nothing. Or was it just the flatness she felt because she was flying home after the memorial service for Eugene? She had, she recalled, sat still and motionless, wondering if she would ever really feel again.

'Do you think a helicopter will come and get us out, Missus?' the boy asked her, more sober now. 'Because we can't stay here for ever just you and me, can we?'

She stared in the direction of the snow-covered windows. She did not answer his question, but it echoed in her mind. But where would the helicopter take her? Not to the United States. She had no current visa and in any case the United States was almost buried in snow, the radio said. She would have to do as Robinette said, wait on a sunny island. She would become the custodian of his drug cupboard, editor of his cablegrams, apple of his eye, his long-lost daughter. But was a daughter what he wanted? She turned her mind to thinking of how life might have been with Eugene. She could hear his voice, quiet and distinct, defending one of his clients. One of the many things he had not lived to do. Eugene would have been a champion of freedom and of integration. But then how could you be quite sure that his idealism would have lasted all these years? Would he have become a member of the Ku Klux Klan? Or, even worse, would he have sold his law practice and bought a patch of farm land? You never could tell with a man. Or would he with his nice bright eyes have taken up with a showgirl, like the one he had deprived his father of? You should never judge a man because he was an idealist in the war; you might get a lot of shocks once the shooting stopped.

'Them woolly bastards, we're not taking them,' the boy said. But, as a concession, he agreed he would spread out a supply of hay for them. 'Yes, Missus, and we'll take my snowman and the cat.' He would soar off into the sky in Eugene's flying jacket and he would have Rixon's medal pinned to his breast and he would have his own high-heeled cowboy boots on, he would wear those whatever the Missus said.

'It's six,' Della said. 'Time to see to the animals now.'

He dropped his arm in the middle of a circling gesture and opened his mouth to suggest that he might go this time so that Della could have a rest, but then he thought of the snowbank and he closed his mouth again. He watched Della pulling on a pair of Rixon's socks and then he saw her warming the inside of her wellingtons.

'When the snow goes, Missus, I'm going to earn a lot of money. More money than you've ever seen even at old Rixon's rotten bank. And do you know what I'm going to do with it, I'm going to give it all to you. Then you won't have to work hard and you won't have to go out in the cold anymore. All you'll have to do is to sit at home and rest.'

'Sew a fine seam, you mean.'

She had reached the foot of the bedroom stairs.

'You can sit by the fire all day.'

She pulled the curtain aside. Whilst it was not directly in the line of the snow it felt damp to the touch.

'As soon as I've made a lot of money, Missus, I'll give it all to you.'

'I'll tell you what's wrong with you, Dan, you live in the future. You're so busy making plans for tomorrow, you haven't any time for today. You're always telling me what you're going to do next week or next year. You never do anything now.' She began to climb the stairs and she was aware that he was following her.

He did not want Della to leave him. He stood at the foot of the stairs for a long time after she had gone, kicking absent-mindedly against the bottom step. He was thinking of the things he did not want. He did not want to steal any more cars, he didn't care if he never drove another car. And he didn't want to tear up any more telephones. His head spun: he did not want to drink any more of Rixon's beer, not ever again. And there was another thing he did not want, and he was reluctant to admit it even to himself. He did not want the snow to thaw. He could not fully understand the thoughts that circulated in his brain. He went in to the kitchen and, using the last of the water in the tap, he put the kettle on to boil. He wanted to make sure that there would be a hot drink ready for Della when she reurned. 'And another thing,' he said, addressing one of the beer cans angrily as if it were another person. 'I don't want the Missus to go out there any more.' He crushed the beer can in his strong hands, then, speaking to himself, he said: 'In future you'll go yourself, you lazy pig.' He held on to the beer can, squeezing it so tightly that it became a flattened piece of metal in his hand.

There was no escaping it: all the flesh seemed to have gone from the bull's face. She decided to inject some more of Rixon's penicillin into its flank, though the drug seemed to have had no effect on its cough so far. But, at the same time, the cough, like the animal, was weakening. She injected the penicillin and shuddered as the bull moaned. 'I'm sorry,' she said. 'You know I don't want to hurt you. But I'm beginning to think that I can't bear my life much longer, not if you die.' She knew now that she understood Europa, the maiden in the myth. And, like Europa, she put an arm around the animal's neck, gently, trying to comfort it, adoring it as Europa had done. 'No, if I lose you, there won't be much point in carrying on for me.'

That night a bit of the boy's ceiling did fall in, as he had said it would. He screamed and when Della went in to investigate, he sat up in bed, rubble and rotten pieces of wood scattered in his hair. Della laughed, seeing his indignant face.

'You're always laughing at me,' he complained. 'You wouldn't care if it killed me, would you?'

'You must have been messing about with it. Those bits wouldn't have come down like that if you'd not been prodding at it. Have you been standing on your bed poking it with something?'

[156]

The boy looked straight at her, so angrily that she wanted to laugh again. 'No, I bloody haven't. You don't need to poke at the ceilings in this rotten house. You don't need to poke to make them come down.'

He was looking so directly at her that she knew that he was telling the truth, there was no sign of his sideways look. She could hardly suppress her laughter. She held up the candle so that she could see the damage; part of the beam had rotted away and the ceiling around it sagged. 'Dan, I think we'd better get your bed downstairs.'

The boy looked at the ceiling too and he pulled himself up in the bed and hugged his knees. 'Will the whole roof come in, Missus?'

It was the same question which Della was asking herself, but she did not feel that it was appropriate to say this out aloud. Instead she said: 'No, of course it won't. That roof's been up for a hundred years and it's seen much worse storms than this. The damp is coming in a bit, that's all, bound to in weather like this. I don't want any more chips of wood or any plaster falling on you, you look enough of a sight as it is.' She did not really feel like laughing now, but she made herself laugh a little for his sake: 'Come on now, get up.'

The boy in Rixon's pyjamas and Rixon's medal slid his legs out of the bed.

'Take all your things downstairs, then come back and help me with the bed.'

The boy looked up at the ceiling again. He was quiet as if a question was forming in his mind.

'Be quick,' she said, trying not to give an answer to his silent question.

When he had gathered his things together, she went into her own room, to see if there was any sign of that ceiling coming in but it seemed to be intact. She thanked God. She had been reading farming books when the boy called out to her and they were still strewn on the bed. Although there was a new emergency, the bull was still foremost in her mind. She picked up

[157]

one of the books. Typical of this place, she thought: the only books we have on farming are seventy or eighty years old. She opened one up at a picture of two cows standing in a shaded field near a lake. A peaceful Victorian pastoral scene. She closed the book sharply. What use was it to her? She could hear the boy moving about downstairs. She thought of calling down to him to hurry up, but first she went to the window to look out and she listened at the window, fancying that she could hear the bull's cough from the house. But even the wild wind had dropped. The silence might mean that the penicillin had worked, cleared up the infection and the cough. She looked away from the cowshed and she saw that there was a clear sky, a sky which seemed to hold no further hint of snow. There would be a time when there was no snow, if it came soon enough she could get a vet. She must leave this place in order, she must see to the health of the animals, she must get the roof and ceiling fixed. It was her duty to do all these things before she fulfilled her promise to the old man.

'Missus,' the boy said, from the doorway of her bedroom.

He was holding onto the door with both hands and her candle cast a shadow behind him. He seemed to have grown taller in the last hour or so, but that might have been just a trick of the light or perhaps she had never really looked at him before. She sat down on the vicar's bed, she was a little unsteady.

'Come on, Missus. We'd better get the beds down into the sitting room.'

'Beds?' I said "bed".'

He looked at the old vicar's bed: 'Better get that down too.'

She opened the farm book again and began to search in it. 'Hang on,' she said. 'I've just got to find something in this book.'

'Come on, Missus. My ceiling's coming in.'

'I will in a minute. I just want to see if there's anything in here about a cure for that poor bull. I don't feel that that penicillin is going to work. I might find a remedy in here, a poultice, something like that. Vinegar and brown paper. Why in hell's name, if we have to keep a bull, can't we have at least one up-to-date book on animal husbandry? God save us from economies.'

'Missus.'

She turned the pages hastily, reading the chapter headings aloud: 'What about this: "Rheumatism; Affections in the chest; Kindred ailments; Catarrh; Diseases of the Organs of Respiration." Ah, here we are.'

'Missus, the beds, we're taking them downstairs.'

'Bed,' she said. 'Don't nag me, the ceilings will last a few hours longer, but I'm not altogether sure that the bull will, not unless I can find something in this book.' She read on: ' "Bleeding; dosage with epsom salts; ginger; gentian root." The old man would be in his element with these: "Insert a seton in the brisket; administer a mild aperient; febrifuge medicine." What's a seton, I wonder and where in God's name is the brisket? "Distension of rumen; fermentation of food taken in the clover field." That bull hasn't been near any clover. "Choking on a piece of turnip impacted in the oesophagus." Turnip in the oesophagus? Listen to this, Dan. Listen. "Symptoms: coughs and moans, refuses food, breath fetid. If untreated, death ensues." ' She stood up and looked at the boy. With the changing light he had become a child again.

'Missus. What are all them words you're saying?' His voice was like a child's voice, filled with tears. 'I don't know what you're talking about. You just go on and the roof will come in and smother us.'

'Yes, I know, I know. But listen to this: "Insert hand in rumen and encourage vomiting." Now what is the rumen? Ah yes, it tells you here. It says: "Force required. Open oesophagus." It doesn't tell you how, of course. "Remove obstructing body." Simple; nothing to it.' There was little information in the index but she read through it hopefully: ' "Purgatives; Scouring; Vomiting; Redwater; Cowpox Drop; Slipping; Warping." ' She was gaining faith in the antique book and she looked at the spine to find the identity of the man who had written it years and years ago: W. W. Porteous. A man like that would understand old farms like this. He understood what it was to run a farm without mechanization, with rusting ancient implements and with no money. And best of all he knew about animals first hand.

She heard the noise of something falling: 'Come on, Missus.'

'Yes, I will. Sorry. My mind is on that bull.' She followed him in to his room and saw that the whole bed was covered now with fine dust and more, larger splinters from the beam, and she thought how the whole house might be wiped out, and they might be wiped out with it. The whole building might disappear in to the ground like Pompeii. But all she said was: 'Dan, I'm beginning to think this house won't ever be the same again.' The farm might be the subject of a dig hundreds of years from now; the photographs, the ambiguous telegrams from the old man, Hugh's letter and his book, the copy of *Ivanhoe*, the boy's fancy cowboy boots would all find their way into an exhibition. The dry bones of the bull would be dug up and wondered at. There was little else that was representative of the age; crushed, old-fashioned furniture; an out-of-date tractor, a museum piece already; ancient ploughs and harrows and hoes. 'We'll take the mattress down first, Dan, then we'll come back for the frame.'

'I can sleep on the mattress on the floor downstairs, can't I?'

She considered this and then she said: 'We don't know how many nights it will be before we get back to normal and you'll be better sleeping higher off the ground.' But truth to tell there was little draught in the house, which was densely packed by snow.

The boy rolled up the blankets and sheets and threw them down the stairs. He was going to throw the mattress after them but Della stopped him. 'Look, it's no use doing that. You're not saving any time, go down and pick those bed clothes up or we're going to break our necks on them.' The boy stuck out his lower lip, but even so he did not disobey her. When he came back they lifted the bedframe and approached the stairs with it.

'Sideways,' Della said. 'Otherwise it's going to ruin the wall.'

'I'll go first, the one who goes first must be strong.'

'Not on your life. The one who goes first must be sensible. The first one does all the manoeuvring.'

The boy stopped dead, so that the bed frame jammed at the top of the stairs, so that neither of them could move: 'Why are you always saying I've no brains?'

'Because you never show any signs of them,' Della said.

'I've got more brains than you.'

No doubt, Della thought. Would I be here with him if I had any brains at all? The boy twisted the bed frame so that he could go first. He dragged Della with him. She pushed from the other end: 'I warn you, if you do any damage, you'll pay for it.'

He bared his teeth at her: 'Nagging old cow,' he said. He tugged at the frame so that she was nearly dragged off her feet; she heard the tearing of the wallpaper.

'If you had your way,' she said, 'there'd be nothing left standing in this house. I'm not surprised your Auntie Millie won't have you. That magistrate was right. He said you were a hooligan and you are!' She reached out, trying to hit at him but there was too much of the bed in between. 'You've no respect for anything. I papered that landing myself so that it'd be nice when Hugh came home at Christmas and look at it now. You don't even say you're sorry.'

'I'm not sorry.' But he spat on his finger and tried to stick the paper down.

'You don't think that's going to do any good, do you? You never take care of anything. All you're interested in is destroying things. What about those cars and telephones?'

There was some difficulty in getting the frame downstairs, it jammed at the point where the stairs twisted near the bottom. The boy stood up straight to rest his back. Then he pulled suddenly, ravaging the paper and the paint: 'Can't get it down without tearing your rotten papering,' he said.

'You did that deliberately. But when the snow goes, you and Tom can live here on your own, you'll not even notice it's a pig sty. Either of you; you're both the same.'

He pulled the bed frame into the sitting room, pushing

[161]

furniture aside to make room for it. Then he laid the mattress on it and lay down, arms folded, legs stretched out.

'What about my bed?' Della said.

'I thought you said you'd stay up there.'

'Yes, well I've changed my mind.'

'Well, you can bring it down yourself. I'm not being bossed about any more. You're always on to me.' He pulled one of the blankets from the floor and covered himself with it.

'What if I get crushed to death?'

'Good riddance for all I care.'

'Well, if you don't mind living in this house with a corpse. If you think you could stand the idea of me lying there dead as a door nail like that Mrs Thompson was.'

He flung the blanket to one side.

'They say that if Mr Thompson hadn't hanged himself, there's no doubt but that he'd have died of fright.'

'Bloody all right,' he said.

The bull looked at her very warily, but she read some kind of welcome in its eyes. Its coughs and gasps were weaker still. She approached it and touched it with a finger: 'You man animals, you're all the same. You always come to us for sympathy. As soon as you have an ache or pain where does all the swaggering go? And it's a good thing I'm still at the farm. What will you do when I'm gone, when you've only got Tom and Dan? What will the three of you do? When I've high-tailed it out as Eugene would say?'

She held the candle up. Light flickered in the navy blue of its eyes, then the eyes closed.

'There's something new I have to do to you,' she said. 'Don't be frightened, will you? I don't think it will hurt. But I don't suppose you'll like it even so.' She put the candle down and with her hands forced the bull's mouth open, recoiling at the stench of its breath and at the blood and mucus which stained her hand. 'Don't move: I've told you I've got to do this.' The bull seemed too weary to protest; it let her wedge open its mouth with a piece of wood. 'I've got to do this, Pride. Even if it's the very last thing I ever do.' Then, in spite of the foul breath, in spite of her disgust and fear, in spite of her own tiredness, she obeyed the instructions in the old farming book and thrust a hand into the bull's throat and down and down and down. Darker blood seeped from its mouth and stained her cuff. The flabby rumen shuddered and then, at last: 'God bless you, Mr Porteous,' Della said.

'I wouldn't worry about that, Dan,' she told the boy. 'After all, what does it matter what happened in the orphanage. That was all years ago. The things the boys said then can hardly hurt you now.' Her mind was on the moment when she had removed the rancid wad of food from the bull's throat. She was triumphant, but she reminded herself that the credit for saving the bull's life in no way lay with her. All the credit belonged to W. W. Porteous. She savoured his name. What did the W. W. stand for? 'William Wilberforce', no doubt. A man who had died years before she herself was born. 'You see,' she told the boy. 'I've tried to explain to you over and over again how necessary it is to learn to read. That's the only way you can take advantage of other people's experience. That W. W. Porteous who wrote that book, he's been dead for years and yet he can still speak to me.' He had reached out of the grave and put knowledge and skill into her hands.

'Them big boys pinched all my stuff.'

'Things get lost when you're a child. In fact, even now I put things down and then when I come to look for them, they're gone.'

She had often complained to Rixon because they had no up-to-date books on agriculture. Nothing more modern than treatises on poulticing, bleeding and herbal cures. Rixon said he had no intention of doing his farming from a book. But she was glad now that she had had to rely on W. W. Porteous.

'This is the most valuable possession I've got,' she told the boy. 'It's the best thing I've ever come across. I'm going to take

[163]

it with me wherever I go. It tells you everything you need to
know about farming and animals. The books today are all too
specialized.'

'I never could have anything, Missus. Them lads took
everything away.'

'Put the kettle on, Dan. Let's have a celebration cup of tea.
I'm worn out. I'm glad we've got my mattress down. Don't
think I could climb those stairs again.' She ran her finger down
the injured spine of the farming book. 'After we've had a cup of
tea I'll read you some bits out of the book, if you like.' There
were advertisements at the end of the book for bicycles with
gutta-percha tyres, washing machines composed of dolly tubs
and mangles, patent cures for cancer, rubs for rheumatism and
varicose veins. 'Maybe *I* should try those rubs.'

'My Uncle Charlie brought me a birthday present once.'

'A birthday present? Your Uncle Charlie pushing out the
boat?'

The bull would be up on its feet in the morning. Freed of the
foreign body, gaining strength and energy and beef.

'I can't wait to see the bull up and about again. Do you
remember how terrified I used to be? I daresay I shall be again
when I see it galloping about. You'll have to treat it with respect,
there'll be no holding it.'

The boy stood up: 'Them buggers pinched everything I got.'

She yawned. 'All that was a long, long time ago. Let's think
about today. Tell you what, I don't want tea. I'd like some
nice cocoa—'

'They even pinched that present that my Uncle Charlie
brought.'

She sat down on the edge of her mattress on the floor,
yawning again, fatigued: 'I'll get you a nice present once we're
out of here. I'll send you one from the island where I go.'

'Bloody thieves.'

She stretched out her legs, then she said: 'When you've
boiled that water, save a little of it, will you. I'll have to wash my
hands and face like a real surgeon. I'll get undressed whilst

you're making the cocoa, and I'll drink it in bed.' She undressed very slowly because of her tiredness. She was happier than she had been for weeks. She wanted to be quiet so that she could think about the ecstasy she had felt when she had drawn out the wad of food and flung it into the snow. She lay back on the old vicar's mattress and pulled the clothes up to her chin so that she would be completely covered when the boy brought her drink in.

'Bloody robbers, all of them.'

'Yes, Dan. But I wish you would forget about them after all this time.' She took the cocoa from him and she sat up to drink it with the sheets still up to her chin. The boy snuffed out the candle with his fingers. 'Oh dear. I was going to read to you. I thought you'd like to hear a few bits from the farming book.' But she was glad of the darkness. She drank her cocoa.

The boy had got his own way about sleeping in the same room as her, but it seemed to have made his temper even worse. She sipped the cocoa. There was a slight stale taste to it. Had he poisoned it? But the taste wasn't surprising when you thought of all the processes the water had been through: vapourizing, freezing, melting, boiling. She drank it greedily, however, telling herself that sometimes life wasn't altogether bad.

'Bloody, rotten thieves.'

She sighed or yawned again; she had not remembered to wash her face and hands. She would have to get out of bed to find a match to light the candle which he had just snuffed out.

'I'm telling you, Missus. Them lads should have been put in jail.'

'Yes, well, let's not talk about them now. I want to think of pleasant things for once.'

'You don't care about me, do you? I bet you're glad them thieves took my things.'

She stubbed her toe on the leg of a chair. 'I wish you wouldn't put the candle out until I tell you. It's pitch dark in here.'

'You wouldn't care if they came here now and pinched my cowboy boots.'

'Dan, for God's sake, stop talking about them will you. And, if *you're* so moral, what about you when you stole those cars?'

'I borrowed them, that's all.'

'What's the difference?'

'I'm not a bloody thief.'

'No, a thief is always someone else.'

She put her cocoa cup down and found the candle and lighted it. The boy lay hunched up in bed, his face turned to the wall. She saw that there was a stain on this ceiling too. Perhaps the whole house was collapsing, but she was too tired to care.

The bull would sleep soundly tonight. Like all young animals it would recover rapidly. The wound would heal, the infection disappear. It was full of penicillin, a drug undreamed of by W. W. Porteous, but that would contribute a little modern knowledge to his cure. The bull would become aggressive and unseeing again, but in some part of its mind it would remember her, like that lion whose bonds were gnawed to freedom by a mouse.

'Missus—' the boy said.

'Please, go to sleep, Dan.'

'You're a mean, ugly bitch,' the boy said under his breath and then he said aloud: 'And if that Western Union Man could see you, he'd get an awful shock. If he saw your wizened up old face just once, he'd never send you telegrams again.'

Della climbed back onto the old vicar's mattress and pulled the clothes up round her. And then with her mind full of happy dreams about the bull, she fell into a deep untroubled sleep.

❧❦

When she awakened she was still happy.

The boy was asleep. At least he did not snore as Rixon did. He slept as quietly as Hugh or as Eugene. But if Eugene had lived, would that state of affairs have gone on for ever? Eugene was twenty-six years old when that shell got him, four years older than Hugh was now and ten years older than the boy.

Eugene might have developed all the habits of the middle aged. She reached her hand out and felt at the double mattress, empty of Rixon and empty of Eugene, empty of the vicar and of his son who had been born on it. The vicar's son was like Eugene and old Sir Edmond, a ghost, so far as she was concerned. But today she did not intend to think of ghosts, she did not intend to feel lonely or unhappy. She felt like a young girl again, a girl who has a bright day in front of her, a day when she will go out in nice new clothes to meet a boy. She got off the vicar's mattress and pulled her old dressing gown over her shoulders. Modesty made her congratulate herself that she had wakened earlier than the boy. She pulled a loose button from her dressing gown, she would sew it on later. Or maybe she would not. She would get a new one as part of her new wardrobe for her new life.

The boy's bare feet poked out from under his eiderdown. The feet were all of him that she could see. They were surprisingly shapely, well formed, like the feet of the martyrs in old paintings. The great toe, unlike hers and Hugh's, was slightly shorter than the rest. Just as it should be according to the Old Masters. She pulled the eiderdown in place to cover up his feet. Asleep, he looked presentable. Asleep, he did not annoy her with his questions and complaints.

The snow she had brought in the night before had melted. She boiled a little of it on the primus to wash herself. She promised herself that as soon as she joined the old man she would take to spending hours and hours a day floating in soft water, but she could put up with this privation until then. She dressed in a pair of clean jeans and a clean blouse and sweater she had put out the night before. Europa and her maidens had dressed in diaphanous robes soaked in water to make them cling to their bodies. But she would tell the bull that blue jeans would have to do. Then she put on a jacket which she had bought new on her last trip to town. She looked at herself in the glass. Her hair had grown too long, partly from neglect and partly because Rixon liked women with long hair. She pulled it back from her face, tempted to cut it short with scissors there

[167]

and then, but she resisted. Before she left the country she would have it cut short in one of the new styles which all the boys and girls now wore. She was not as sure as she had been that she would stay with Robinette permanently. The bull's survival had weakened her resolve. But if Rixon wanted to keep her he'd have to mend his ways. 'I want a new roof, a new regime, a door and a corridor so that in future we've got access to the animals from the house. I want a new life, if I'm going to stay,' she'd say. There'd be no climbing out of windows, never any more. They'd make a bonfire of all this furniture, particularly the vicar's bed. She would be nicer to Tom, but he'd have to be nicer to her too. He'd have to understand that she was tired of being a slave. They'd have to do something for the boy, take him in hand. Get him that television book, for one thing. Make sure he learned to read. She would get his crooked teeth improved. A boy like him could be straightened out these days. They'd do something about the water supply. If they could get a license to milk, they could give the bull a real role in life.

She switched on her transistor to see what was happening elsewhere in the world, but as she had feared might happen, the battery was dead.

She told herself: There's one thing, there isn't really anything that can go wrong now, unless the house falls down on my head. But the dark patch on the ceiling did not seem to have become any worse. There was still the boy's transistor. He had played it non-stop ever since the television went off, he had insisted that his batteries were superior and that they enjoyed long life. She took it from his bedside and switched it on at low volume. She tried to light the fire with wood too damp to ignite, and as she struggled with the snow-layered coal. She tried to turn the transistor up but could get little more volume than on her own: someone was giving an eyewitness account of an explosion, but she could not tell where it had been. The name of the place escaped her: when you were snowed in the rest of the world seemed too far away to bother about. That battery, she thought, is dying. 'Long-life' did he say?

It seemed that she heard someone forecasting a thaw, but that might only be wishful thinking on her part. There was something else about people dying in their cars in snow-drifts; she shuddered, wondering where.

She scattered handfuls of sugar on the fire to make it go. Rixon would disapprove of that, of course, but she had had enough economy. 'And another thing,' she would tell him, 'I've made my last coal fire. Get electric radiators fixed or central heating. From now on our lives must be cold-proof.'

She warmed her hands. Then she switched stations on the transistor and heard the sound of several people singing; the words 'true love' were chanted over and over again. True love: why were people who sang songs so naïve and optimistic? She switched off to conserve the battery; if the boy's transistor went they'd have no contact at all with the big, bad snowless world.

She propped the shovel in front of the fire and put a newspaper over it to make the fire draw. The editor had used up a whole column of print to tell his readers what a great year this was going to be. But they were warned of a potato famine in the second column and galloping inflation in the third. The paper scorched and caught fire and for a few seconds the room was illuminated by it, but then it blackened and died. She reached for the cat: 'There's one thing, Moggie, if this snow goes, I'll stock up with batteries and firelighters and paraffin. I never want to run out of heat again.'

She rose; it would be a good idea to clean up the house, what there was left of it to clean. The boy, in spite of all his promises, had not done the things he had said he would. She went towards the vacuum cleaner automatically, but then, remembering, she sought out a dustpan and a brush. 'I know I'm crazy,' she told the cat, 'there'll be more rubble and more water before the day is out, but today I want to keep the flag flying. My motto is: "I'll carry on".' Her feet were light as she climbed the stairs.

The boy woke up and searched for his transistor with his hand. It was not there where he had put it. He felt around for it, swore under his breath. Then he screamed for Della: 'Missus. Missus. Somebody's taken my transistor. Everything I have gets pinched.'

She came back down the stairs.

He was walking around the room in her husband's pyjamas. No buttons on the jacket were done up and there was a new tear in the sleeve. Why couldn't he take care of other people's possessions? After all, he made enough fuss about his own.

'Some bloody burglar's been in here and nicked it.'

'Nobody can get up here. *I* borrowed your transistor, if that's all that's troubling you. My battery's finished and I wanted to get the weather forecast, that's all.'

'Where is it?' His hands snatched. 'Give it to me; it's mine.'

'Go easy on it, it's our only contact now.'

'I don't care about the weather.' He held the transistor to his ear and tuned in to the dying strains of a guitar. He shook it and the guitar failed.

'You've bloody done for it.' He approached her with the transistor like a weapon in his hand.

She moved to one side. 'Dan,' she said, 'it's bad enough being cooped up in here with you without you going on like that.' She faced him. The hand holding the transistor fell. 'Now I'm going to get your breakfast. You can get washed and I'll put some more of Mr Rixon's clothes out for you, you look as if you've been down a coal mine. From now on we'll have some standards around here.'

'Well, I'm not getting washed.'

'I don't want any quarrels.'

He looked down at his transistor.

'I've nothing to listen to, no one to talk to, nowhere to go.'

'Do something useful. We'll get on with your reading lessons. The bull might be dead now if I hadn't been able to read what Mr Porteous said.'

There was a faint flicker of interest: 'I'd rather write than read.'

She began to feel hot and feverish. Her feeling of well-being was disappearing. 'Reading and writing are the same thing.'

'My Uncle Charlie said they're not.'

'How can I quarrel with the oracle?'

Could she have caught something? Some germ? Was such a thing possible in all this snow? 'We'll worry about that later,' she said. 'In the meantime, let's try to make the best of things. Keep ourselves occupied as best we can.'

'I'm still not getting washed.'

She wiped her forehead with the back of her hand. What did it matter whether the boy was clean or not. 'You do as you like. I'm going out to see the animals.' She stretched. 'I think in future I'll stick to animals. They're always glad to see you. They never answer back.'

The boy was busy taunting the cat with a piece of bacon from his plate. The cat mewed and dug its sharp claws into the chair.

'Dan, please, don't tease it.' She cut off a rasher of bacon and gave it to the cat. 'I'm glad we've got some bacon. After this week I wonder if I shall ever touch beef again.'

The boy began to sing one of his pop tunes in his tuneless loud voice. 'Women are no use,' he sang.

'I don't think I've heard you sing that song before,' she said. 'There are some horrible songs around these days: "Creepy as a snake. Ugly as a toad." For Heaven's sake. What kind of words are those?' The boy sang on. 'I'll tell you what I did like. I liked those songs you and Hugh were singing at Christmas. Both of you together, you sounded really nice.' Hugh's baritone had drowned out the boy's lack of tone.' Why don't you sing one of those?'

He said: 'I can't remember any of them songs.' Then he smiled and began to sing a song which she had never quite caught on to: 'Bio'? 'Bayou'? 'Bayeaux'? What was it? The melody was good and she even found herself joining in, singing just a word or two. 'Dan,' she said, 'what is that? What exactly is it you're singing? I can't quite make out that word. What is it? "Bio"?'

The boy moved nearer to her, so near that he almost touched her; she watched his shadow moving in the candlelight. 'Do you like me?' he asked.

The question disconcerted her. Like: what did he mean by that word? Was this a child's question? Or was there some more serious intent; something more sophisticated? She could not see the expression on his face and she turned and kept her eyes on his shadow, as if she were conversing with it and not the boy.

'Do you like me?' he said again.

She tried to laugh. 'Would I put up with all your nonsense if I didn't?'

'You haven't much choice now we're snowed in here.' His shadow moved nearer to her and his arm almost touched hers.

'I could go out and live in the cowshed, couldn't I? I could go and sleep with the bull.'

'That bloody bull.'

His words, the very words that she had often used herself to Rixon, startled her.

She said: 'I always thought the bull was a friend of yours.'

'I hate the bloody thing,' and now his shadowy arm did touch the shadow of her arm. The elbows interlocked and formed a dark triangle against the wall. She moved away from him.

'It's strange,' she said, at last. 'I don't dislike the poor bull at all now. I've stopped being annoyed about the money it cost. It depends on me so much ever since the snow. When things depend on you you get fond of them, responsible. You start to like them—' She had been going to say that when things became dependent on you you started to love them, but 'love' struck her as a dangerous word to include in her vocabulary. The boy lay on his bed, making animal shadows with his fingers on the wall: a dog, a bear, an elephant. It was a skill he must have

[172]

learned somewhere. At the orphanage maybe. He listened to everything she said, weighing her words and then he said: 'Do you like me, Missus?'

'I've told you,' she said and her voice was a little nervous now. He gave her his secret sideways look and she moved the candle so that his animals were destroyed but his face illumined. She saw now that he smiled at her openly as if she had become his friend at last. A friend just like the bull.

'Say that you like me.'

'Daniel, don't be so silly.'

Then he began to sing his song again.

' "Son of a gun, we'll have some fun————" '

He stopped and then he said: 'Hugh said it was your song.'

'My song. That's a funny thing to say. I don't even know the words.'

'He said it was written especially for you.'

'He was teasing you.' Her hand which held the candle was not quite steady. 'You take everything he says seriously.'

'He said: "You know what's wrong with my mother, Dan?" He said: "She lives in the past She spends all her time looking back—" '

'Hugh would never say such things.'

'He did, Missus. I swear.'

'No, Daniel, I don't believe you.'

'He did. He said: "My mother lives in her memories." '

She put down the candle and buttoned up her jacket. 'I can't imagine Hugh saying things like that. I suppose I do live in the past a little. Every mother does. You don't forget your child's childhood. Hugh used to have terrible teething trouble, I've never seen a baby suffer so. He used to cry and cry with pain. Then when he got a bit older he was always quarrelling with his father. I used to pray that they'd start to get on better. I can remember every word they used to say. Then poor Hugh didn't really like going to school at first, my heart bled for him every day when I had to leave him there. He was all right when he got older, but you don't forget things like that.' Hugh and his spots,

Hugh and his difficult friendships. Hugh and his desperation to keep up with the lord's son. Were those the memories he was talking about? Was that what he meant by living in the past?

'He told me it a lot of times. He said: "We can only guess where your mother is, Dan, but we always know where mine is. She lives down Memory Lane. Way Down Upon the Swannee River." He did, Missus. Honestly.'

She remembered the way Hugh had of dredging up lines from songs to punctuate his conversation.

'He said it was about time you changed your tune.'

'I suppose he made a suggestion.'

' "Down on the Farm", he said.' The boy took in a breath—

'Don't bother to sing it. I've had enough of your music for one day.' She thought about the past which Hugh despised. What did he hate about it? Eugene and his cinder body too burned to be brought back to the States? The Sunnyside Motel in Tennessee where the old man shed tears for his dead son and the long journey home without Eugene? The little happiness she had had in those days? Was that the past which Hugh was tired of hearing about? Were those the memories he begrudged her?

'Hugh said them telegrams was crazy and that old man had softening of the brain. He said he was going to put a big red cross on the calendar so that you'd remember what year it was.' They both looked at last year's calendar which should have been taken down.

'Hugh said when he was little, he didn't like his dad going away, Missus. He said it was awful because you made him sleep in your bedroom. And then he had to listen to your snoring.' He imitated Hugh's imitation: ' "Scubble, scubble, scubble." '

Hugh, she recalled, had had whooping cough once and he had begged her not to leave his side. She remembered the disturbing noise he had made.

'Scubble, scubble, scubble. Old Rixon says you're like a pig.'

'You're going too far—' There was very little water left but even so she washed her cup with great care. Then she inspected it, scrutinizing its base and rim as if a great deal depended on its cleanliness. 'I'm going to see the animals. You come up to the window so I can hand some fresh snow in, then you'll be all right whilst I'm out. And tonight, instead of torturing each other, let's have a feast to celebrate the saving of the bull. We'll take all the best food out of the freezer and we'll have a treat. Thank God, the food's still safe. We'll have all your favourite foods.'

He picked up her cup and breathed on it, then polished it, turning it round as if it were something rare, something he had never seen before. 'Do you really like me?' he asked.

She took the cup from him: 'I've just washed that. Don't breathe on it.'

'Do you?'

'Why do you keep asking me?' She took down the calendar and threw it in the bin. 'I try to, Dan. But you make it very hard.'

He snatched the cup and drew a cross on the inside of it: 'Do you know what old Rixon said to me and Hugh one day?' And now his voice was sly. He set the cup down suddenly. Della shivered at the sound. '"Take my advice and never marry a widow woman," he said. "It's the biggest mistake I ever made. And if you must marry a widow woman, marry one who doesn't snore."'

She faced him. 'Did Mr Rixon say that?'

'Said you lived in a graveyard; said you sounded like a sow.'

The clock struck. It was not the electric clock, of course, and it was not the old grandfather clock which had come from Della's home. It was a shabby mechanical clock which Rixon had picked up somewhere. It was the only thing still going in the house. 'Well, well,' she said.

The boy licked grease from his fingers and he looked at her, expecting some more violent reaction to his words. There was a slight pain in Della's chest, a pain which had become more frequent since the snow. She sat down on the vicar's mattress and counted up her injuries: a cut leg, a pain in the side, a varicosed vein, several grazes, sundry bruises, bones chilled by the snow, pride shattered by the boy.

[175]

'And where the hell's the marmalade for my bread?' she heard him say. She got up steadied herself and handed him a newly opened jar.

He stabbed into it savagely with his knife: 'I don't like this kind you made. I like that nice kind you get from shops. This is all full up with skin.' He spread it very thickly on his bread.

'Well, we'll have a lovely meal tonight, I promise you: strawberries or raspberries? you decide.'

'You can chuck them to that bull.'

She dusted the crumbs that he had made.

'And don't give me any of that meat mucked up with wine.'

He licked his knife, something she had told him that he must never do and then with his crooked eyes he looked straight at her. 'Me and Hugh was talking about you one night and I said I wished I had a mother.' He put his knife down on his plate, blade turning in as she had taught him to.

'Dan, you mustn't be jealous of Hugh,' she said. 'It's natural we should be close.'

'Hugh said: "You orphans, you don't know when you're well off." '

His fingers now played tunes upon his arm.

She felt at the place where the calendar had been. Strange, this year they had received no calendars at all. She would have to buy one to cover up the space.

'He said he didn't blame his dad for that other woman.'

A calendar was, of course, a reminder of the fleetingness of time. When you saw those three hundred and sixty-five days all laid out, you were impressed by how few days there were in a year. She must not get one of those calendars which showed you the whole year at a glance. It was better not to be reminded of the way time flies. What have I got to show for the years I've already had? she asked herself.

'He said his dad needed another woman. It was the only way he'd ever get a bit of peace from you.'

She went upstairs and looked out of the bedroom window. The

[176]

sky had changed, but there was still that unfathomable turquoise light. She might have been looking out at an alien landscape on some other planet, newly discovered, somewhere gripped by a long ice age. She looked at the strangeness of the colours of the cloud and at the brilliant band of light which separated the earth from the sky.

The boy's voice came behind her: 'Missus, all them things I said—'

She felt cold now, much colder than she had felt at any time since the first fall of snow. Could there be some inner frozen core which had been brought to life and which was struggling to get out? She began to prepare herself for the climb out of the window. How many times was this? She thought as she slid down the icy snowbank that she would always have a debt of gratitude to the bull, because the bull was the only thing on earth which needed her. She landed with a crash, lamenting that there would be more bruises and more scratches. But a few more scars would make very little difference.

The things the boy had said to her had made her heart heavy. It was hard to recapture the feeling of hope. But, as she opened the door of the bull's shed, a little of the optimism came back as she prepared herself to meet the bull again. He would be completely restored to health by now. He would be weak, yes, but on his feet, full of life, breathing, waiting. To hell with Hugh, she thought. Why should I care what he thinks about me any longer? And to hell with Tom. If he has another woman, she's welcome to him— And then, like a young girl, she straightened her shoulders and brushing back her hair with a hand she stepped forward, her feet displacing the clean straw she had put down for the bull.

Mr Porteous had led her up a gum tree.

There was no point in weeping, she had learned that over the years. She had learned that lesson only too well in that period in the past which Hugh said he was tired of hearing about. Tears got you nowhere. She knew that the only thing to do in times of adversity was to whistle a happy tune and carry on. 'Do what you have to do,' she shrieked out to the turquoise air. Follow the yellow brick road, even if it was temporarily frozen over. She looked at the house but then turned her back on it. As she walked away from it, she saw the boy's snowman and she circled past it.

She came across more bodies of sheep and those of a few lambs. Some were buried, but others lay uncovered, lying dead where the wind had blown the snow away. She put out as much food as she could for the ones which were still alive and she handed food to the horses, feeding them by hand. But the fact that they were living did not compensate for the fact that the bull was not. She might have ridden one of the horses to make her escape more easy, but she felt a strong desire to get away from them, to be on her own. She did not let the dogs out because she did not think at this moment that she could bear their exuberance. Instead she handed food in to them, ignoring their barks of greeting. 'Dan will climb out when I don't come back, he'll let you out later. He'll be glad of your company then. He'll see you get your supply of fresh snow.'

Fresh snow: not water. Even your vocabulary changed in weather such as this. You were like a cosmonaut, adapting to changed circumstances. But there was little fresh snow to see, unless you struck out from the house; around the house it had become darkened, tarnished, filthy. There was nothing new about it. If you wanted fresh snow, the kind she had just promised to the dogs, you'd have to go further afield, perhaps in the direction she was going. But the provision of food and drink for the animals was not her responsibility any longer. She set out, just as the boy had done, walking towards the west. The going was not easy; a thickish film of ice now covered the snow. There was none of the powderiness with which the boy had had to contend. Instead a hard glazed surface on which her feet slipped and slid. But she walked on. Eventually there would be an end to all this. If you walked far enough, you'd come to a better clime.

The boy peed out of the window. He made a golden arc in the sky which pierced like lava into the snow.

'You don't like me doing that,' he said. 'Do you?' He spoke aloud, as if Della were standing by the window at his side. 'It's another of my filthy habits and you said that if I did it again, I'd have to go.' He looked out of the window towards the cow-sheds and he imagined Della in there, talking to the bull. 'Well, you'll have to catch me first, won't you? And when you're in making a fuss of that bloody bull, you can't see what *I'm* doing, can you?' He laughed again: 'So there!'

She would walk until she came to the end of the snowdrifts and then she would find another farm, somewhere warm and dry, somewhere with a telephone that worked and she would put through a call to Robinette, calling him collect because she had no money. Her cold fingers counted out the words: COMING BACK TO YOU DADDY, she would say. Although she planned to speak to him personally, she found it easier to visualize the words in capitals on strips of paper, the medium by which his messages came to her. IVE DONE ALL THE THINGS NORMAL WOMEN ARE SUPPOSED TO DO IN THE WAY OF BEING A GOOD WIFE AND MOTHER STOP IVE READ ALL THE MAGAZINES ON INFANT AND CHILD CARE STOP IVE BEEN A CHATTEL LOVED AND HONOURED AND ON THE WHOLE OBEYED BUT FROM THIS DAY FORWARD MY LIFE HAS GOT TO CHANGE. Because of the form it had taken, she relayed her message sparely in as few words as she could. WHAT YOUVE ALWAYS WANTED HAS HAPPENED DADDY STOP MY SECOND MARRIAGE IS IN SHREDS MY SON HAS FLOWN THE COOP AND I AM RARING TO RETURN TO THE FOLD IN FACT IM ON MY WAY. She did not turn back to look at the farm. What use was there in that? Ahead of her she could see no landmarks. She could not even see the nearest

[179]

neighbouring farm situated directly to the west. She did not want to meet people she knew; she wanted to go to some strange, unknown farm. Her breath became frozen as she walked and cold air stung her lungs. She tripped over tree roots, hidden mounds of earth and once she stumbled and fell on the rotting body of a sheep. Sometimes she almost had to crawl because the going was so rough. Her steps became slower as she walked and stumbled on. There was still, she saw, that strange turquoise in the sky. Snow had got into her boots and she sat down against a tree and pulled one of them off so that she could shake it out and straighten up her sock. Of course, if I actually do telephone him, she thought, I needn't economize on words at all. I will simply tell him how terrible my life has been. I'll have to be getting on my way. Resting will get me nowhere, I've got a very long way to go— She struggled up again; her clothes, she found, were partially coated with wool from the dead sheep she had fallen on.

The boy gave the cat a saucerful of food, bread soaked in milk which was reconstituted from powder and melted snow. He did not seem to have the heart for teasing any more. Instead he stroked the cat's head with one of his big fingers and then he stroked its paw.

'Do you like me?' he asked the cat, putting his ear close to its lapping face. But what could a cat say? It looked up and then from side to side to see if there was any danger which might attack it whilst it ate its food. Spots of milk powder incompletely mixed stuck to its whiskers. When it saw that it was safe it began to lap again.

'You don't care about me do you?' he said. 'Nobody does.' But he did not seem to be talking to the cat, he did not seem to be talking to it at all. He was talking to someone else. 'Moggie, do you know where that crazy old Della is?' He stood up and laughed. 'She's in there with that bull. She's always in there giving it medicine and sticking needles in it. She says she's saved its life, I expect she'll stay with it all night. Crazy witch.' He wrapped his long arms round his neck, scratching at a spot with a little finger. 'She's nuts the way she goes on about that bull. She didn't even like it at one time; she hated it. She was always saying so and now it's: "Poor bull this, poor bull that—" Moggie? Do you know what she did to that bull? She put her hand right down its filthy throat.' He lay on the floor and opened his mouth wide so that the cat could have seen down his own throat if it had not closed its eyes and drawn its head into its body. 'She's still in there, messing about with that rotten bull, stroking it and giving it things to eat. And she can't even bear to put a finger on me.'

She had got quite a long way from the farm by now and at times she felt that she might reach the end of the snow. Ahead of her there was a ploughed field which someone had prepared in the autumn for winter barley. She looked at the neat ruled lines of snow and earth, of white and brown. The furrows were a relief from the continuous glare of the past days. She walked forward quickly towards the field, but suddenly fell awkwardly on a piece of metal which had been covered by the snow. She swore a little because of the intense pain in her foot. If she had not been too tired and too cold, she might have taken her rubber boots off, but she did not even think of this. Perhaps it had been a mistake to come this way. She struggled on a little further until she came to another tree; her foot had begun to swell and the pain was too great to let her go any further. She moaned a little, but there was little use in crying out when you were all alone. She sat down against the tree, trying to choose the dryest spot. Perhaps it *had* been a mistake to come this way, perhaps she should have gone towards the road, but she remembered she had wanted to head west. Am I crazy? she wondered. She leaned back against the tree, putting her injured foot into the most comfortable position she could find. Sleepiness overtook her in spite of the pain. Before she fell sound asleep, she heard herself say one last thing: 'It's a pity but now this has happened I haven't a chance of ever seeing him again.' But she was too tired to inquire of herself who the 'him' she spoke of might be.

The boy leaned over Della's body and shouted out to her: 'Missus! Come on. It's no good lying there. You'll catch your death of cold.' He took hold of one of her cold hands and rubbed it to try and get some life back into it and then he breathed his own warm breath on her. The dogs, who had found her first and had licked the first snow from her, circled around, barking in the frozen air. The boy saw that droplets of ice had glued her eyelids together and he tried to separate them with his big fingers. 'Please, Missus,' he begged her. 'Don't be dead.' He thought of Mrs Thompson and he wondered how she had looked when the postman and the Varleys found her. He wondered if her face and lips had been pale and if she had slumped as awkwardly as Della in her chair or bed. He did not know whether Della was still alive. His years of watching shoot-ups on television had not taught him how to differentiate between life and death. He looked at her and felt sad; he felt sadder than he had ever felt before since the social worker brought him to the farm. He stood looking at her for a few minutes and then, because he felt a need to do something, he picked her up in his strong arms and carried her back to the house, finding his way by following the footsteps he and the dogs had made in the hard surface of the snow.

It was difficult to talk to Della: in the cold air he needed all his breath, but he felt some need to let her know in words, whether she could hear him or not, that he had missed her in the hours whilst he had waited for her return: 'You never ought to have left me, Missus. You never should have gone.' The dogs ran too close to his feet, almost upskittling him. 'Get out of it you devils,' he yelled. 'You'll make me drop her, carrying on like that.' Then again he scolded Della. 'That magistrate said: "Dan, your only hope is to find some nice woman who'll be a mother to you." What did you leave for? You've no right to go walking out on your son.' But, in spite of his resentment and in spite of the fact that he chid her with neglect, he did not feel the burden of her on his shoulders as a burden at all. The proximity of her body to his was comforting to him: 'You've no right to go wandering off in weather like this without telling me,' he said. He adjusted his position a little, standing to snatch a moment's rest. The discovery that she weighed so little frightened him; he resolved to walk more quickly in case the cold winds should somehow manage to blow her away.

He toppled her gracelessly on to the old vicar's mattress and then laid her out gently in case he had damaged her. He put all the blankets from his own bed on to her and then he put his arms around her and rocked her for a while. He tried to feed a spoonful of Rixon's brandy into her cold mouth, but saw it dribble back onto her chin.

'You shouldn't have paid no attention to all them things I said.' He rubbed her cheeks to get the blood to flow back into them. 'You know I tell lies all the time. You're always saying I make things up.' He placed the pillows nicely for her. 'Missus, I wish you'd wake up and talk to me, I wish you would.' Then he left her so that he could fill hot water bottles for her. 'And all them things I said your Hugh said, Missus. I said to him: "Hugh you ought to be ashamed of yourself." ' He put the hot water bottles into place against her stomach and her legs. ' " Talking about your mother like you do." ' He placed the cat at her side, instructing it to keep her warm: 'You stay there, Moggie. Don't you dare jump off.' Then he approached her gently and put his hand against her heart, willing back its beat. 'I mean it this time, Missus. Things will change; I'll never let you go out in the snow on your own any more. I'll clean the cows and I'll feed the bull. I'll put my hand down its throat and fish things out when they get stuck. I'll get the water and I'll clean the house, I'll scrub and polish till my hands drop off.

[183]

And if your Hugh doesn't want to come here any more, I'll stay with you and be your son.' His mouth was against hers and his warm breath poured into her between his words. 'And,' he looked a little to one side, 'you can have my bloody transistor if you want, you can keep it for ever if you like. I won't be mean with it again.' He reached for it and put it to her ear. 'I've warmed up the battery, you can hear it now.' There was trouble in Rhodesia and there was likely to be more. President Carter had made a hopeful speech. In spite of that, however, food prices were going up and no one seemed able to bring them down. Someone had defused a bomb in a building seconds before it was due to explode. 'And don't you go worrying about your Hugh. Don't think about him and his toffee friends. And don't you believe what I said about old Rixon and that woman; I made it up, Missus, honestly, I did. And don't worry about him getting all your money any more.' He searched his mind for other words to comfort her and he searched her body for signs that she was still alive; he spread the large fingers of his big right hand against the cool nakedness of her left breast, pressing until he elicited a sign of life. 'I won't be nasty to you, Della—not any more I won't. And I'm sorry for all the things I've said. I'd do anything for you, you know that. I'd give you everything I've got.' His hands took hold of her body and pulled it close to him. He had offered her all his possessions, but apart from his cowboy boots and the transistor, which he had already parted with, he had surprisingly little to give, except the life force which flowed in an even rhythm from his large young body as it lay covering hers, moving slowly on the mattress of the old vicar's discarded bed.

The thaw began on Monday and the boy brought weak tea to Della whilst she still lay in bed.

'It'll turn to water soon and then it'll all run away.' She

stirred her tea, wondering what might happen to the stones and beams of the old house when once that happened. She wondered what desolation might follow a shifting of the snow. 'They'll come racing back,' he said. 'Rixon and your Hugh. You'll see.'

She sipped her tea.

'I've been upstairs,' the boy said. 'I've been outside as well. There are some of the ridge tiles off and a few of the others as well. It might not be so bad when it all dries out.'

He had put a liberal amount of sugar into her tea, because he had seen a programme on television which said that sugar provided energy and heat. She drank, trying not to mind. She had stopped taking sugar during the war and she thought of telling the boy that, but the war, she decided, was too long ago for him to care about.

She watched him, drinking his own tea from a mug, not holding the mug by the handle but clasping his hands around it, though there was no longer any reason for his hands to be so cold. The thaw had wrought a temperature change.

She said: 'After all this time, I'd begun to think the snow would never go.'

'Do you know what I wish, Della?'

He toasted a slice of bread at the fire for her to eat with her boiled egg. 'If it wasn't for that bad foot of yours, I'd wish there wouldn't be a thaw—'

When they had both eaten their breakfast, he wiped crumbs from his trousers and then went upstairs to the bedroom window to slide for the last time down the softening bank of snow.

The boy spotted the Land-Rover when he was standing at the door. He kicked the sodden blankets to one side and went in to the house.

He had already dragged his own bed upstairs and now he dragged up the mattress from the vicar's bed. Inevitably it made more tell-tale tears on the wallpaper on the landing. 'He's back,' he said to Della. 'Rixon; somebody's brought him in a Land-Rover. I told you it'd not be long before he got here.'

[185]

Della was rebandaging her foot, treating it carefully to avoid the pain. 'Did you tell him I was in here?'

'No, I came straight in, I didn't speak to him.' She looked at the face of Rixon, a young stranger on the mantelpiece.

'He'd think that was funny, wouldn't he? His Number One avoiding him.' She tucked in the end of the bandage and limped to the door. The sun was bright and the glare from the snow hurt her eyes. She shaded them.

'Hello,' Rixon said. He seemed to be stiff and he stretched his legs as if he had been travelling in the landrover for hours and hours. He gestured and she saw that Marsden the postman was driving and that a young girl was in the middle place. 'I've tried all ways to get up here, Della. The roads are like a sheet of ice. But Mr Marsden said he could manage it in this, so I cadged a lift.' He began to examine the mounds where the boy had piled up the bodies of the dead sheep and lambs. 'I see there have been a lot of casualties,' he said. 'Well, I suppose that's only to be expected in a siege.' She suspected that he might like to know the final toll, so that he could estimate the extent of his loss, but this thought did not distress or anger her. It seemed to her that this was a time for taking stock. The postman climbed out of the driver's seat. She was as surprised by the extraordinary thickness of his brows as she had ever been. She nodded. Her mind switched to the outside world. What letters and cables had he been hoarding since the snow? Where was he hiding all her cables, the lavender envelopes from Auntie Millie, letters from Hugh announcing his intentions about the secret Bee?

'New car?' was all she said.

'I got delivery of it three days ago. Just in time for your old man. He'd never have got up here without me.' She saw that the postman was looking at her damaged foot and she wondered if he was thinking of Mrs Thompson who had damaged her foot in the last big snow. She wondered if the postman would ever forgive her for having stayed alive? She considered if she ought to ask him if he had brought a spade.

'You've had a bad time,' Rixon said.

[186]

'Oh no, it's been a laugh a minute.'

'I've been looking round,' the postman said. 'And it'll cost a pretty penny to get this place back in shape. You'll have to dig deep into your savings.' When he said this he looked straight at Della. 'And then with all these animals you've lost.'

'Animals?' Della said and her mind was full of the bull. 'Yes, you haven't seen everything yet.'

'Better look at the cows.' Rixon began to walk over to the cowsheds and she limped behind him followed by the postman.

'A little more slowly,' Della said and she took Rixon's arm, 'I can't keep up this pace. Besides I want to put off the moment when you see poor Pride.'

'Pride?' Rixon said. Could it be that he had forgotten his great love?

'That cough; you remember, don't you? Well, it got worse and worse. It's all been a terrible calamity. That was the worst thing that happened in the whole week.' The postman stopped to tickle the nose of the lamb with a straw.

'Pride,' Rixon said again and there was no way of knowing what he was thinking. He might not reveal anything of that until the postman had gone, but then he said: 'It's odd, when I came back I felt sure it'd be the old lame cow that would have gone—' He lifted up the heavy cowshed door. 'That one there—' he indicated to the postman which cow he meant.

The postman grinned and approached the cow. 'No,' he said and he looked at Della as he spoke. 'That lame cow'll last a long time.' He looked closely into its eyes. 'There's a lot of life in that old lass yet—'

The boy had climbed up into the driving seat of the Land-Rover. The girl was telling him about the controls. Everything was new to him. His face was set and there was no sign of his sideways look. His hands gripped the steering wheel.

'My God,' the postman said. 'I've only had that thing three days. Better get that lad out of there or I'll be walking home.'

'No,' Della said. 'He won't do any harm—' She looked straight at the windscreen and saw the faces of the boy and girl, un-smiling, side by side. The boy spoke briefly to the girl and then he avoided all their eyes as his long legs swung out of the driving seat.

'Hugh phoned every day to see if there was any news of you.'

'Did he? He was probably wondering if I'd used his book for fuel.' She looked beyond Rixon to where the boy stood on a slight hill near to the dry stone wall. He was too far away for her to see the expression on his face.

'Oh yes, and I phoned Auntie Millie dutifully to put her in the picture and I heard the life story of every goldfish in the tank. Did you know that every one of them has a separate personality? And that they are more rewarding than children? They get to know you and then they're grateful for every ant's egg you give them. And also you haven't to take notice of Uncle Charlie when he phones. He has an ulcer and he's jealous of the fish.'

They both went in to the house and she watched Rixon step over the piles of blankets and she saw him test the hinges of the door. It had become so warped that there was a danger it might never close again. She saw him look at the place on the floor where the vicar's mattress had been and then up at the damp patches on the ceiling. She went into the kitchen and began to heat a pan of melted snow; soon there would be running water again.

'Maybe I'd better do what you want, Dell. Get rid of this place. I know you've never liked it here. It's what I've always wanted, but it's not really any use to you.'

'I don't think there's any point in talking about such matters, Tom.' She looked at the door, wondering how soon it would be before the postman wandered in. 'Not until we're alone anyway—'

'The trouble is, there's something else. Something more serious I have to say—'

'Go on then, say it, if you must.' So there *was* a woman. The boy had retracted the story, but she had known that it was not a lie. 'First-hand. Straight from the horse's mouth. Let's have it. Major Rixon addressing his troops.' I hope I don't laugh, she thought. 'Go on, Tom.' He had taken a batch of blue-winged envelopes out of his pocket and he arranged them carefully in his hand as if they were a fan of playing cards. So he knew then: it was a case of tit for tat. He would go off with his new lady and she would go back to old Robinette as she had promised to, back to the comforts of Mimosa Street.

'You've read them?' He had always said that letters and cables were sacrosanct.

'I thought you'd want me to.'

'Yes, I suppose you hadn't a lot of choice.' Eavesdroppers, she thought, tend to hear no good—

He was keeping the confessions of a bank manager till later then. First he was going to tell her that he knew she planned to desert him and to run away. He would explain to her that he understood. All is forgiven, he might say. He would tell her the price she must pay for gaining her freedom from him a second time. He would put gentle pressure on her to change her mind. Or perhaps, if he felt strongly about his new lady, he might put gentle pressure on her to go. Some of the amused affection she felt for him touched her now: 'Come on, Tom, say it. I know you know. You needn't worry about mentioning the subject to me.'

The water in the pan was boiling; if he did not speak soon it would all boil away and then she would have to start all over again. She could see out of the windows now where the snow which had covered them had melted away. She must go and get the boy, call him in, she must offer a drink to the postman and the girl, thank them for bringing her husband home. She must remember to tell Rixon what an asset the boy had been, diligent, courageous, resourceful, the saviour of the day. She must secure his future, now that there were doubts about her own.

'Tom,' she said and she put a wifely hand on Rixon's arm, 'I shouldn't take the cables too seriously. You know what the old man is and how he exaggerates. He's always had the most preposterous plans and, for some reason, he's never got over the idea that he owns me. As a matter of fact, I think he's right to communicate by telegram. It's exactly the right medium for him. Sufficient room for ambiguity. He's never really ever trusted the telephone. He's like George the Fifth, he always calls it the "electric telephone". ' She moved a little closer to him: 'Half the things he says in the cables are said off the top of his head. I don't think he gives them any thought. He'll go on sending cables to me, one or two a day until the day he dies. If I really did go back as he's always saying he wants me to, I wonder if he'd be glad or not. There'd be no one left for him to send cables to.' She put out a hand for the envelopes. 'So come on, let's get it over. There are lots of very important things we've got to do.'

She felt his fingers tighten on the envelopes as if he were afraid to let them go.

'The cables have become a habit with me. They're a kind of escape into the past, a bit of a relief from everyday life. You had your farm and I had the feeling that however tough things were I'd still got a foothold in Mimosa Street. I expect I need those cables as the bit of fantasy in my life—'

And now he did hand them over, but then he said: 'Della, I'm sorry but it's all come to an end. The escape hatch has just shut. That one isn't from the old man. I knew as soon as I read it that it wasn't his style at all. If old Robinette could have written his own obituary cable, he'd never have economized on the stops.'

The boy had discarded Rixon's medal but he was wearing the new grey hand-knitted socks.

'You won't be leaving here then, will you?' he asked Della.

She walked by his side, still limping on her painful foot. The snow had been made slushy by the recent sun and rain. Like Rixon she tried to estimate what had been lost in the storm and what had been gained.

'You won't be going off to that old man?'

His housekeeper would have arranged a nice little lying in state for him at the funeral parlour. It would not even be possible for her to go to that. 'No, Dan. There'll be no ride in the rodeo, not for me.'

He flung a stick for the dogs and they watched the dirty mud splash. 'I don't suppose I'll ever go to America now either,' he said. The dogs came racing back, barking for more sport. The retrieved stick was laid at his feet.

'Look,' she said. 'Your snowman, it's still there.' She saw Hugh's scarf still tied around its neck. 'I'm afraid its days are numbered, Dan. There's no hope of it lasting now the temperature's shot up like this.'

The boy looked around him and then walked over to the dry stone wall: she tried to walk faster to catch up with him, wondering what he had found. He bent down to pick up a lamb, abandoned by its mother. 'Better take it inside, see if I can warm it up,' he said.

'Yes, well, so much for Mr Rixon and his staggered breeding season. The only thing on this farm not about to give birth is the cat. Lambtime in January. What a year to choose.'

The boy walked more slowly, carrying the shivering lamb. 'Did you and Mr Rixon decide whether I'd be staying on?' he asked.

She looked up at the roof of the house, at the gaps where the tiles were missing and at the holes where the beams were exposed and she looked at the jagged spaces in the gable end. It came back to her that she had once run out of the house in Mimosa Street and that she had jumped into a passing taxicab. She told the driver to drive her to the airport and 'step on it'. She couldn't bear the thought of being late, because she was meeting Eugene on what turned out to be his last trip home.

'You the English nanny or sump'n?' the cab driver said.

She could remember the hot sun on the azalea bushes and the suffocating Spanish moss.

'Do I look like an English nanny?'

'You sound like one.'

'You don't think I could be the mistress of the house.'

'No ma'am. The white people who comes outa them houses is mostly swells. They kinda look like they belong.'

'I think the cab driver was paying you a compliment,' Eugene said, when she told him about it. 'I wouldn't want to think I'd turned you into a Mimosa Street matron, I can tell you that.'

But it was no use remembering all these things now, it was no use remembering Eugene. And it had not been Della Rixon that cab driver had been speaking to. It had been someone young and very pretty, prettier by far than that girl in the Land-Rover, someone with the whole of her life before her, someone lithe and fleet of foot, an occupant of another world, a world long gone by. She looked up at the fractured farmhouse which was now her home. 'That house you came outa,' that cab driver had said. 'I'm telling you, it ain't no shack.'

'What are you talking about?' she asked the boy. 'You don't think you and me stand a chance of escaping from this place, do you? Not a hope. We've been sentenced for life. Hard labour too.' She smiled at him and once again she tried to see him as a young girl might, that girl today maybe. Not the young Della perhaps, not the girl who had been stolen from Rixon all those years ago, but some more ordinary, plainer girl. 'No, come to think of it, I'm wrong. One of these days some girl will come along and set *you* free. But I'll never get away, not now. I'll just stay here with Mr Rixon and make the best of things.'

Rixon, she saw, was walking around the buildings, estimating the cost of the repairs, calculating the damage that had been done to his life by the snow.

'I don't see some old girl coming and getting me,' the boy said.

'The trouble with this life is, it's all a case of wait and see.'

She tried to smile at him and he smiled back, then once again he began to walk too fast for her, quickening his pace so that she was left behind. Then he began to dance, turning three circles with the lamb held to his breast. She watched his big, not quite straight frame as he went on rapidly towards the house, carrying the lamb as carefully as he had carried her.